I like it like that

a gossip girl

novel

Gossip Girl novels by Cecily von Ziegesar:

Gossip Girl
You Know You Love Me
All I Want Is Everything
Because I'm Worth It
I Like It Like That
You're the One That I Want
Nobody Does It Better
Nothing Can Keep Us Together

I like it like that
a gossip girl
novel

by

Cecily von Ziegesar

LITTLE, BROWN AND COMPANY

New York ❦ Boston

If you like this book, you may also enjoy:
Maximum Ride by James Patterson
Twilight by Stephenie Meyer
The Dating Game by Natalie Standiford

Little, Brown and Company

Time Warner Book Group
1271 Avenue of the Americas, New York, NY 10020
Visit our Web site at www.lb-teens.com

First Edition

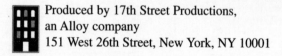
Produced by 17th Street Productions,
an Alloy company
151 West 26th Street, New York, NY 10001

ISBN 0-316-73518-3

10 9 8 7 6 5 4
CWO
Printed in the United States of America

No gossip ever dies away entirely, if many people voice it: It too is a kind of divinity.

—Hesiod, ca. 800 B.C.

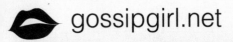
gossipgirl.net

topics ◀ **previous** **next** ▶ **post a question** **reply**

Disclaimer: All the real names of places, people, and events have been altered or abbreviated to protect the innocent. Namely, me.

hey people!

Thank you one and all for coming to my party last week. I would have written sooner but honestly, it's taken me this long to recover. I realize it *was* a little crazy to have a party on a Monday night, but didn't the week *zoom* by afterward?! I'm pretty sure you're all still trying to figure out if I was the skinny blond girl in the emerald green Jimmy Choos or the tall black guy with the amazing sapphire-blue fake eyelashes. And it was so sweet of you to bring me gifts—especially the adorable caramel poodle puppy—when you didn't even know who I was! The truth is, I kind of like being an international woman of mystery, so for now, I'm going to keep my identity to myself, frustrating as that may be. Think of it as a diversion from the *endless* days of waiting to find out if we got into college, a distracting puzzle to piece together while we endure the stress and boredom of these bitter March weeks.

Not that we really need diversions. We've got plenty to entertain ourselves with—gorgeous couture clothes, huge Upper East Side apartments *with staff*, various "country" houses and holiday retreats, limitless credit cards, pretty diamonds, hot cars (although most of us don't even have our driver's licenses yet), and doting parents who let us do absolutely whatever we please as long as we don't embarrass the family. Plus, spring break is just around the corner, giving us lots of free time to get *busy*.

Sightings

S walking up **Madison Avenue** drawing mustaches over her face in those gorgeous poster ads for **Les Best**'s new perfume,

Serena's Tears. B in **Sigerson Morrison** on **Prince Street,** indulging her shoe fetish. **N** depositing a shopping bag filled with rolling papers, roach clips, bongs, pipes, and lighters into an East Eighty-sixth Street waste bin. **D** smoking a cigarette on the subway platform at Seventy-second Street and Broadway late at night, challenging the transit cops to arrest him and provide him with some much-needed new material for his poetry. **J** with her new best friend, **E**, and boyfriend, **L**, poking around the Chelsea art gallery district—pretty darned sophisticated for a bunch of ninth-graders. Wait, I think he might actually be in tenth—does anyone really know *anything* about that guy?? **V** and her rocking big sister dumping garbage bags on the sidewalk outside their Williamsburg apartment building. Spring cleaning? Or maybe **D**'s dead body all cut up? Ew! Sorry, that was nasty.

Your e-mail

Q:
Dear gossipgirl,
so I'm getting frustrated that ur like never going to tell who u r. r u? cuz i'd really like to meet u in person. who knows, maybe i already have! so far i think u have basically admitted that ur a senior girl who goes to constance. right?
—qrious

A:
Dear qrious,
I'm not going to go ahead and give you my home address right here and now, or even tell you what grade I'm in. If you were cool enuf to be at my party, you might have seen me, although usually I'm so completely surrounded by my . . . entourage, it's hard to even get a glimpse. Stay curious, though. Eventually you might find me out.
—GG

Q:
Dear GG,
Are you hot because if you are not, it's going to be really tough for you once everyone knows who you are. Like, she was just some jealous ugly girl!
—wise

Dear wise,
You don't even know the meaning of hot until you've met me, which you most likely never will.
—GG

Now about that *thing* that's been secretly nagging more than a few of us . . .

To go to college a virgin, or not?

Do we do something about it now, with a boy we've known for years? Do we get rid of it over spring break? Over the summer? Or do we settle into our dorm rooms just as we are, bold but innocent, and ready to lose it with the first campus player to say, "Come hither"? Maybe we should just listen to our mothers and older sisters and "wait till the time is right," whatever *that* means. Of course some of us girls nipped this particular issue in the bud long ago, opting to spend our college years focusing on more important things, like geology and Freud. *Not.* Face it, even if you're not a virgin anymore *now*, you're going to feel like one all over again the minute you step on campus. And that's a good thing.

Thanks again for my presents! Big smoochies—you rock!

You know you love me.

gossip girl

there's no place like home

"What island are we going to, anyway?" Blair Waldorf asked her mother. Eleanor Waldorf Rose was perched on the edge of Blair's bed, watching her daughter get ready for school while they discussed spring break.

"Oahu, dear. I thought I told you. We're going to that resort on the North Shore, so the boys can learn to surf." Eleanor cupped her hands around her almost-seven-months-pregnant belly and frowned at the cream-colored walls as if trying to channel the baby's preference about wallpaper. She was due in June, and Blair would be off to college soon afterward. Today Eleanor and her decorator would discuss her plan to turn Blair's room into a baby girl's nursery.

"But I've already *been* to Oahu," Blair wailed dramatically. She'd known for weeks that they were going to Hawaii for spring break, but until now she hadn't thought to ask where. She kicked her antique mahogany dresser drawer shut and stood in front of the full-length mirror on the back of her closet door, primping. Her close-cropped brown hair was neatly tousled; her white cashmere V-neck was just deep enough to suggest a hint of cleavage without her having to worry about being sent home by Mrs. M, the headmistress, for dressing like a slut; and her new turquoise Sigerson Morrison flats looked so excellent with bare legs, she decided not to put on tights, even though it had been an unusually frigid March and she was going to freeze her ass off. "I want to go someplace *new*, " she added, pouting into the mirror as she applied a second coat of Chanel lip gloss.

"I know, sweet pea." Her mother slid off the bed and squatted down to eyeball a particularly dangerous-looking electrical outlet in the skirting board near the window. Once the decorating was finished she would have top hire someone to baby-proof the entire house. "But you've never been to the North Shore. Aaron says the surfing is the best in the world."

To Blair's dismay, her mother was wearing beige velour track pants with the word *Juicy* on the butt.

Hello, inappropriate?!

"So do I, like, not exist anymore?" Blair demanded. She dragged her baby blue shearling Dior saddle bag out of the closet and dumped her school stuff into it. "First you're kicking me out of my room, and now I have no say about where we go for vacation?"

"The boys are buying some surfing things for our trip right now. You might want to have a quick look on Aaron's computer. See if there's anything you want," her mother answered distractedly. She was on her hands and knees now, circuiting the room, checking for any dangers that might be lurking from a baby's point of view. "You know, I *was* thinking apricot for the color scheme—so it's girly, but not too pink? But now I'm thinking maybe a greeny yellow might be even nicer. *Endive*."

Blair had had enough. She didn't want to go to the North Shore of Oahu, she had no interest in buying surfing equipment, she didn't want to talk about color schemes for the stupid baby's nursery, and she certainly didn't need to look at the word *Juicy* on her mother's wide-load, pregnant ass for a moment longer. With a final spritz of her favorite Marc Jacobs perfume, she left for school without even saying good-bye.

"Yo, Blair. Come here a minute!" her seventeen-year-old stepbrother yelled from his room as she stomped by.

Blair stopped and poked her head into the room. Aaron and her twelve-year-old brother, Tyler, were sharing Aaron's natural-fiber desk chair—all brotherly—while they ordered surfing gear online with Cyrus Rose's credit card. Tyler had stopped combing his hair in an attempt to grow dreadlocks just like Aaron's, and he looked as if he had some sort of foul hair fungus. Blair could hardly believe this was the room she was going to have to live in until she went off to college. Aaron's hemp bedspread and natural sea-grass carpet were littered with old reggae album covers, beer bottles, and Aaron's dirty clothes, and the room stank of his herbal cigarettes and those revolting soy hot dogs he was always eating—*raw.*

"What size are you?" Aaron asked. "We can order you a wet shirt. It keeps the board from chafing."

"They come in cool colors," Tyler added enthusiastically. "Neon green and stuff."

Like Blair would ever be caught dead in neon green, let alone a neon green wet shirt.

She could feel her lower lip trembling with a mixture of horror and overwhelming sorrow. Here it was, only seven forty-five in the morning, and she was already on the verge of tears.

"Found 'em!" Cyrus Rose, her eyesore of a stepfather, boomed from behind her. He waddled down the hallway from the master bedroom, wearing only a red silk bathrobe tied with a dangerously loose knot. His bristly gray mustache needed a trim, and his fat face was red and oily. He waved a pair of enormous orange swim trunks at Blair. They had little blue fish printed all over them and would have been kind of cute on anyone but him. "Love these. Boys are going to order me a wet shirt to match!" he announced happily.

The idea of spending Easter break watching Cyrus make a fool of himself on a surfboard wearing his orange swim trunks and a matching orange wet shirt was enough to drive Blair to real tears. She slunk away down the hall to the foyer, yanked her coat out of the coat closet, and hurried off to meet her best friend. Hopefully Serena would think of something— *anything*—to cheer her up.

As if that were even possible.

s has a stroke of genius

Serena van der Woodsen sipped her latte and squinted gloomily down at Fifth Avenue from her perch on the steps of the Metropolitan Museum of Art. Her abundant pale blond hair overflowed the hood of her belted white cashmere sweater coat and spilled onto her shoulders. There it was again on the side of the M102 bus—the ad for Serena's Tears. She had no problem with the way she looked in the picture. She liked how the cold wind had whipped her yellow sundress up between her St. Barts–tanned knees, and how even though she'd been wearing only sandals and a sundress in the middle of Central Park in February, the goose bumps that had studded her arms and legs had been carefully airbrushed out. She even liked how she wasn't wearing lipstick, so her perfectly full lips looked sort of chapped and bruised. It was the tears in her enormous dark blue eyes that bothered her. Of course that was what had caused Les Best to name his new scent Serena's Tears in the first place, but the real reason Serena had been crying in the photo was because that was the day—no, the very *minute*—Aaron Rose (whom she was pretty sure she'd been in love with, at least for a week) had broken up with her. And what bothered her, what made her feel like crying all over again, was that now that they were broken up, she had no one to love, and no one to love *her*.

Not that she didn't love almost every boy she'd ever met, and not that every boy in the world didn't totally love *her*: It was impossible *not* to. But she wanted someone to love her and shower her with attention the way only a boy who was *completely* in love with her could. That rare sort of love. *True* love. The kind of love she'd never had.

Feeling uncharacteristically dark and melancholy, she pulled a Gauloises cigarette from out of her rumpled black corduroy Cacharel bag and lit it just to watch it burn.

"I feel as ugly as the weather," she murmured, but then broke into a smile when she saw her best friend, Blair, walking up the steps toward her. She picked up the extra latte she'd bought, stood up, and held it out. "Kick-ass shoes," she remarked, admiring Blair's latest purchase.

"You can borrow them," Blair offered generously. "But I'll kill you if you spill anything on them." She tugged on Serena's sleeve. "Come on, we're gonna be late."

The two girls ambled slowly down the steps and up Fifth Avenue toward school, sipping their coffee as they went. Cold wind blasted through the bare-limbed branches of the trees in Central Park, making them shiver.

"Jesus, it's cold," Blair hissed. She tucked her free hand into Serena's white cashmere sweater-coat pocket the way only a best friend can. "So," she began to vent. She'd gotten control of her tears, but her voice was a little unsteady. "Not only does my mother walk around, like, stroking her ovaries, but today the decorator is coming to turn *my* room into Baby Central, in shades of radicchio and *ass*!"

All of a sudden, Serena's longing for true love seemed kind of trivial. Her parents hadn't gotten divorced because her dad was gay, her middle-aged mom wasn't pregnant, her stepbrother hadn't come on to first her and then her best friend and then ditched them both, and she wasn't being forced to move out of her room. Not only that, she wasn't still a virgin at the grand old age of seventeen, and she hadn't kissed her Yale interviewer and then almost lost her virginity to her Yale *alumni* interviewer, completely messing up her chances of getting in. As a matter of fact, when she really thought about it, her life was just peachy compared to Blair's. "But you get Aaron's room, right? And it's just been redecorated for him—it's nice."

"If you like hemp curtains and ecofriendly ginkgo-leaf furniture," Blair scoffed. "Besides," she added, "Aaron is an idiot. Going to Oahu for spring break was totally his idea."

Serena didn't think Oahu sounded so bad, but she wasn't about to contradict Blair when she was in a bad mood and risk getting her eyes poked out. The two girls crossed Eighty-sixth Street against the light, banging against each other as they ran to keep from getting mowed down by a taxi. When they reached the sidewalk, Serena suddenly stopped in her tracks, her huge blue eyes gleaming excitedly.

"Hey! Why don't you move in with *me*?!"

Blair crouched down to hug her frozen bare calves. "Can we keep moving?" she asked grumpily.

"You can live in Erik's room," Serena continued excitedly. "And you can totally screw Oahu and come skiing in Sun Valley with us!!"

Blair stood up and blew into her coffee, squinting at her friend through the steam. Ever since Serena had come back from boarding school Blair had completely hated her, but sometimes she totally loved her. She took one last sip and tossed her half-empty cup into a trash can. "Help me move in after school?"

Serena slipped her arm through Blair's and whispered in her ear, "You *know* you love me."

Blair smiled and rested her trouble-weary head against Serena's shoulder as the two girls turned right on Ninety-third Street. Only a few hundred yards beyond stood the great royal blue doors of the Constance Billard School for Girls. Ponytailed girls in gray pleated uniform skirts milled around outside, chattering away as the notorious pair of seniors approached.

"I heard Serena got a huge modeling contract after she did that perfume ad. She's going to bring her baby back from France. You know, the one she had last year before she came back to the city? All the supermodels have babies," chirped Rain Hoffstetter.

"I heard she and Blair are going to get an apartment downtown and raise the baby themselves instead of going to college. Blair decided not to *ever* have sex with guys, and obviously, Serena has had enough sex to last her whole lifetime. Just look at them," intoned Laura Salmon. "Total lesbos."

"I bet they think they're making some big feminist statement or something," Isabel Coates observed.

"Yeah, but they won't feel so good about it when their parents are, like, forced to *disown* them," Kati Farkas put in. The first bell rang, summoning the girls into school.

"Hey," Serena and Blair called over as they passed the group of girls on their way inside.

"Cool shoes!" Rain, Laura, Isabel, and Kati sang back in reply, even though only Blair was wearing new shoes. Serena was wearing the same old scuffed brown suede lace-up boots she'd been wearing since October. Blair always had the best shoes and the best clothes, and Serena always looked gorgeous, anyway, even in her frayed, cigarette-burned boarding school clothes. Which was yet another reason to hate the pair, or to love them, depending on who you were and what mood you were in.

the only unbaked boy on the lax team

"Got it!" Nate Archibald twirled his lacrosse stick over his head, scooped up the ball, and tossed it expertly to Charlie Dern. His flushed cheeks were smudged with dirt, and his golden brown curls were matted with sweat and bits of dried Central Park grass, causing him to look even hotter than the hottest Abercrombie & Fitch model in the entire catalog. He lifted his shirt to wipe the sweat from his glittering green eyes, and even the pigeons roosting in the trees nearby cooed with pleasure at the sight. The group of junior girls from Seaton Arms watching on the sidelines tittered with excitement.

"Whoa. He must have worked out a lot in prison," breathed one girl.

"I heard his parents are sending him out to Alaska after graduation to work in a tuna-fish cannery," said her friend. "They're worried he'll go back to dealing drugs if he goes to college."

"I heard he's got this heart condition that's really rare. He has to smoke pot so he won't have attacks," said another. "It's actually kind of cool."

Nate flashed them an oblivious grin, and the girls

simultaneously closed their eyes to keep from falling over backward. *God*, he was perfect.

It was the beginning of the season and no team captain had yet been appointed, so each boy was on his best behavior. After their usual scrimmage, Coach Michaels had asked them to free-throw for a while. Nate was throwing with his friend Jeremy Scott Tomkinson when he heard his cell phone ring in the pile of coats. He signaled to Jeremy and then sprinted over to answer it.

Georgina Spark, Nate's girlfriend of several weeks, was currently residing in an exclusive drug-and-alcohol-rehabilitation facility in her hometown of Greenwich, Connecticut, and was only allowed to make supervised phone calls at certain times of the day. The last time Nate had missed her call, she'd been so bummed out, she'd gone on a bender and had later been found on the roof of the clinic, chewing Nicorette gum and sniffing a bottle of nail polish remover, both of which she'd stolen from a nurse's purse.

"You're panting," Georgie observed coyly when Nate answered. "Were you thinking about me?"

"I'm at lax practice," he explained. Coach Michaels spat noisily into the grass only a few feet away. "I think it's just about over, though. Are you okay?"

As usual, Georgie ignored the question. "I love how you're all athletic and healthy and chem-free, and I'm sitting in this jail, pining for you. Just like a princess in a fairy tale."

Or not.

A few weeks earlier, Nate had been busted by the cops while buying a bag of weed in Central Park and sent to out-patient rehab at Breakaway, in Greenwich. Nate had first met Georgie in teen group therapy. One night, during a tremendous snowstorm, Georgie invited Nate back to her mansion to hang out. They got baked together, and then Georgie disappeared into the bathroom to pop prescription pills. Soon enough, she passed out in her underwear on the bed, and Nate had had absolutely no choice but to call the people at Breakaway to come get her. And ever since then, they'd been boyfriend and girlfriend.

That would be some messed-up fairy tale.

"So the reason I'm calling is . . . ," Georgie crooned into the phone.

Nate's teammates milled around him, pulling on their coats and chugging from the bottles of Gatorade they'd brought with them. Practice was over. Coach Michaels spat a wad of phlegm near the toe of Nate's sneaker and pointed a gnarly forefinger at him.

"I'd better go," Nate told Georgie. "I think Coach wants to talk about appointing me captain."

"Captain Nate!" She squealed into the phone. "My cute little captain!"

"So I'll call you later, okay?"

"Wait, wait, wait! I just wanted you to know I got my mom to convince these monkeys to let me out starting Saturday, as long as I'm with an adult or responsible mentor, so we're totally going to my mom's ski condo in Sun Valley for your spring break, okay? Will you come?"

Coach Michaels growled something at Nate and put his hands on his old-man hips. Nate didn't have to think about Georgie's question for very long, anyway. Sun Valley sounded a heck of a lot better than regrouting his dad's old catamaran up at their summer house in Mt. Desert, Maine.

"Of course I'll come. Definitely. Look, I have to go."

"Yippee!" Georgie squealed. "I love you," she added hoarsely, and then hung up.

Nate tossed the phone on top of his navy blue wool Hugo Boss coat and rubbed his hands together energetically. His teammates had all gone home. "What's up, Coach?"

Coach Michaels took a step toward him, shaking his head as he sucked in snot from his nasal passages.

Yum.

"Last year I almost made you captain when Doherty crapped up his knee," the coach said. He spat and shook his head again. "Good thing I didn't."

Uh-oh.

Nate's hopeful smile cracked a little. "Why's that?"

"Because you're not captain material, Archibald!" the coach barked. "Look at you, gabbing on the phone like a playboy while the rest of your teammates are out there dogging it. And don't think I don't know about your getting busted for dope." He made a little growling sound. "You're no leader, Archibald." He spat again and turned his back on Nate, jamming his hands in his red Lands' End parka pockets as he walked away. "You're just a rotten pile of disappointment."

"But I haven't been smok—" Nate called after him, his voice trailing off into the wind. The sky was steel gray, and the bare tree branches creaked and moaned. Nate stood alone on the brown March grass, holding his lacrosse stick and shivering a little in the cold. His father was a former navy captain, so he was used to shrugging off the power-tripping tirades of grumpy old authority figures. But it was still pretty outrageous that Coach Michaels thought the only nonstoned guy on the team wasn't fit to be captain. Coach hadn't even given him a chance to defend himself.

He bent down and picked up his coat. If he were stoned right now, he would have smiled serenely at the coach's accusations and lit a joint. Instead, he slung his coat over his shoulders, gave the finger to the coach's retreating back, and trudged across the darkening meadow toward Fifth Avenue.

Charlie, Jeremy, and Anthony Avuldsen were waiting for him on the pathway leading out of the park. Anthony was too much of a stoner even to play sports, except for the occasional game of soccer in the park, but he always met the guys after practice with ready-rolled joints and a big grin on his freckly, blond-goateed face.

Slowly the boys made their way out of the park and onto Fifth Avenue. "Dude, he made you captain, didn't he?" Charlie asked, his voice cracking the way it did when he was high, which was basically all the time.

Nate grabbed the bottle of blue Gatorade out of Charlie's hands and took a swig. Even though these guys were his best friends, he wasn't about to tell them what had happened. "Coach offered it to me, but I turned him down. I mean, I'm pretty sure I'm already into Brown, anyway, so it's not like I need lax captain on my transcript. And I'll probably miss a few weekend games hanging out in Connecticut with Georgie. I told Coach to give it to a junior."

The three boys raised their eyebrows in surprised admiration. "Jesus, dude," breathed Jeremy. "That's like, *huge* of you."

All of a sudden, Nate felt the sort of rush he might have felt if he'd actually told the coach to make a junior captain instead of him. How huge he *might* have been, if only that was what had really happened.

"Yeah, well." He smiled uncomfortably and buttoned up his coat. Not only had he lied about the coach offering him the position of captain, he'd also lied about his chances of being accepted at Brown. Sure, his dad had gone there, and sure, he'd had a kick-ass interview, but he'd been baked as a loaf of bread for every exam and standardized test he'd taken since eighth grade, so his grades and scores were barely mediocre.

"Here." Anthony held out a burning spliff. He had a tendency to forget on an hourly basis that Nate had quit smoking the stuff. "It's Cuban. I bought it from my cousin who goes to Rollins down in Florida."

Nate waved the joint away. "I have a paper to write," he said, turning away from the group toward home. It was hard to get used to—not being stoned. His head was so clear, it almost hurt. And all of a sudden there was so much to *think* about.

Whoa.

d's glass is half empty

When school let out for the day, the formerly scruffy but now fashionably groomed and polished Daniel Humphrey didn't linger outside Riverside Prep with the other senior boys, bouncing basketballs and eating pizza from the slices place on Seventy-sixth and Broadway. Instead, he zipped up his new black APC storm jacket, retied his Camper bowling shoes, and headed across town to the Plaza Hotel to meet his agent.

The ornate gold-painted Plaza dining room was buzzing with the usual throng of gaudily dressed Russian tourists, extravagant grandmothers, and a few loud families from Texas, all toting shopping bags from FAO Schwarz and Tiffany, and all taking high tea. Except for Rusty Klein.

Mwa! Mwa!

Rusty blew kisses into the air on either side of Dan's face as he sat down.

"Is Mystery coming?" he asked hopefully.

Dozens of gold bracelets clanked noisily as Rusty clapped herself on the forehead. "Fuck me! I guess I forgot to mention it. Mystery's on a six-month world book tour. We've already sold five hundred thousand copies in Japan!"

The last time Dan had seen Mystery had been at an open

mike at the Rivington Rover Poetry Club downtown. They'd practically had sex on stage as they performed improv poetry together. Then the wan, horny, yellow-toothed poetess had retreated to write, and Dan hadn't seen her since.

"But her book's not even out yet," he protested.

Rusty piled her fire-engine-red hair on top of her head and stuck a sharpened number two pencil through it. She picked up her martini and guzzled it, smearing hot pink lipstick all over the rim of the glass. "It doesn't matter if the book *never* comes out. Mystery's already a celebrity," she declared.

An avid chain-smoker, Dan was suddenly desperate for a cigarette. But smoking was prohibited, so instead he grabbed a fork from off the table and pressed the tines into the palm of his shaking hand. Mystery, who was only nineteen or twenty (Dan wasn't quite sure), had managed to write a memoir called *Why I'm So Easy* in less than a week. The day she'd finished it, Rusty had sold it to Random House for an astounding six-figure advance, with a film deal attached.

Rusty scooted her chair forward and pushed her half-drunk glass of stale tap water toward Dan, as if she expected him to drink it. "I sent 'Ashes, Ashes' out to the *North Dakota Review*," she told him offhandedly. "They hated it."

"Ashes, Ashes" was Dan's latest poem, written in the voice of a guy who misses his dead dog, only it was left up to the reader to figure out that the narrator was addressing a dog and not his old girlfriend or something.

> *It's the first baseball game of the season*
> *I wait for your kiss*
> *Breath meaty like chocolate*
> *My shoes are still there*

One in your bed where you left it
The other in the backseat of my car

Dan slumped in his chair. The week his poem "Sluts" had come out in *The New Yorker,* he'd felt invincible and famous. Now he felt like a schmo.

"Sweetness, I can think of several reasons why your writing may not appeal to everyone the way Mystery's does," Rusty crooned. "You're young yet, sugarplum. All you need is some good training. Fuck me, I need another drink." She belched into her fist and then stuck both hands above her head. Within seconds, a sploshingly full martini was set down before her.

Dan picked up the half-empty glass of water and then set it down again. He wanted to ask her about those "several reasons" why his writing didn't appeal to everyone the way Mystery's did, but then again, he was pretty sure he knew. While Mystery mostly wrote about sex, Dan mostly wrote about death, or wanting to die, or wondering if being dead was better than being alive, which was kind of depressing if you thought about it. Also, he wasn't an orphan like Mystery was—according to legend, anyway. An orphan raised by prostitutes. Dan was just a seventeen-year-old kid who lived in a sprawling prewar apartment on the Upper West Side with his outrageous but loving divorced dad, Rufus, and relatively loving, big-boobed little sister, Jenny.

"So was that all you wanted to tell me?" he asked, feeling depressed.

"Are you kidding?" Fueled by the fourth gulp of martini number two, Rusty whipped a cell phone out of her limited edition Snapdragon Louis Vuitton purse. "Get ready, Danny-boy. I'm calling Sig Castle at *Red Letter.* I'm going to get him to give you a job!"

Red Letter was the most prestigious literary journal in the world. Started five years ago by the German poet Siegfried Castle in an abandoned warehouse in East Berlin, it had recently been bought by Condé Nast and moved to New York, where it was currently thriving in its role as the rogue avant-garde child of the publishers of *Vogue* and *Lucky*.

Rusty started dialing before Dan even had a chance to respond. Sure, working at *Red Letter* would be an honor, but he wasn't really in the market for a job right now.

"But I'm still in school," he muttered. His agent tended to forget sometimes that he was only seventeen and therefore couldn't meet her for midmorning espressos on a Monday or fly to London on the spur of the moment to attend a poetry reading. Or hold a full-time job.

"Sig-Sig, it's Rusty," she crooned. "Listen, babes, I'm sending you a poet. He's got potential, but he could use a little sharpening up. Got me?"

Siegfried Castle—Dan still couldn't believe Rusty was actually talking to *the* Siegfried Castle—said something Dan couldn't hear. Rusty thrust the phone at him. "Sig wants a word."

Dan's hands dripped with sweat as he held the phone to his nervous ear and croaked, "Hello?"

"I hawen't gut a cwue vho you ahr, but Wuthsty cweated dat vantastic Mystewy Cwaze, so I thuppose I muthst take you athswell, yah?" lisped Siegfried Castle in a snooty German accent.

Dan could barely understand a word, except for the Mystery Craze part. How come everyone had heard of Mystery and no one had heard of *him*? After all, he'd been published in *The New Yorker*. "Thank you so much for the opportunity," he responded meekly. "I have next week off school for spring break, so I can work all day. Once break is over, I can only come after school."

Rusty grabbed the phone away from him. "He'll be there Monday morning," she pronounced. "Bye-bye, Sig-Sig." Clicking off, she tossed her phone into her purse and groped for her martini. "We used to be lovers, but it's better now that we're friends," she confessed. She reached out and pinched one of Dan's pale, confused cheeks. "Aw. You're Sig-Sig's new intern, his cutie-patootie little intern!"

Rusty made it sound so demeaning, as if Dan would be spending his workdays stirring Siegfried Castle's decaf mochas and sharpening his pencils. But an internship at *Red Letter* was such a prestigious, impossible-to-get job, he couldn't possibly complain.

"So, is *Red Letter* named after the letter *A* for *adulteress* that Hester Prynne had to wear in *The Scarlet Letter*?" he asked, genuinely interested.

Rusty stared at him quizzically. "Fuck if I know."

how not to talk to the person you're not talking to

After the *Rancor* editorial meeting, Vanessa Abrams raced out the door of Constance Billard and down the steps. Her hair didn't fly out behind her, bouncing prettily against her shoulders, because she kept her head shaved and basically had no hair. And she didn't have to worry about twisting her ankle in her heels, because she never wore heels. In fact, she never wore shoes, only boots. Big ones, with steel toes.

The reason Vanessa was in such a hurry was because Ruby had given her a list of crap to buy at the health food store on the way home from school, and she really needed to get it done and get home before her parents arrived, just in case she'd forgotten to put away some evidence of her filmmaking and they found it and found her out.

At the bottom of the steps, she nearly mowed down the very last person she'd expected to see. Dan, her former best friend and boyfriend. His light brown hair was neatly styled, with long sideburns framing his serious jaw, and he was wearing a gray suit that looked French and expensive. This from a guy who previously only cut his hair when he stopped being able to see, and who wore the same pair of brown corduroys until the bottoms were frayed and there were holes in the knees.

Vanessa tugged on her black wool leg warmers and folded her arms across her chest. "Hello." *Why the fuck are you here, anyway?*

"Hey," Dan responded. "I'm just waiting for Jenny," he explained. "I got a job today. I wanted to tell her about it."

"Good for you." Vanessa waited for Dan to say something else. After all, he was the one who'd cheated on her with that Mystery bitch, and he was the one who'd completely sold out to become famous. He could at least apologize for *that*.

Dan remained speechless, his eyes shifting from her face to the school doors and back to her face again. Vanessa could tell he was dying to tell her about his new job, but she wasn't going to give him the satisfaction of asking about it.

She pulled a tube of Vaseline out of her black bomber jacket pocket and smeared some on her lips. It was the closest thing to lip gloss she owned. "I saw your sister inside, talking to her art teacher. She'll be out in a minute."

"So what's up?" Dan asked, just as she was about to take off.

Vanessa suspected he was only asking so she would ask *him* what was up, and then he could tell her all about how he'd been nominated for the Pulitzer Prize or some such shit.

"My parents are coming to town tonight," she responded, caving in a little. "You know how much fun that always is for me," she added, and then wished she hadn't. It didn't do any good to remind them both that they knew everything about each other now that they no longer spoke. "Anyway. Bye."

"Yeah." Dan held up his hand and gave her a big smile, the kind of fake, shit-eating smile he'd never even known how to give until he started going to fashion shows with air-kissing agents and famous weirdo-slut poetesses. "Good to see you."

Good to see you too, asswipe, Vanessa responded silently as she strode toward Lexington Avenue to catch the subway to Williamsburg.

Actually, it *was* kind of good to see Dan, and she'd wanted to tell him more. She'd wanted to tell him how her parents' incessant "We are artists, hear us roar" personas stifled every ounce of creativity in her. How her parents didn't even know she made films, even though it was basically the only thing she enjoyed doing. How they didn't even know she'd gotten in early to NYU, purely on the strength of her art. And how they wouldn't know, for the duration of their nearly two-week stay, that her bedroom closet was stuffed with film equipment and her favorite old videos. Ironic though it might seem, Ruby—the kid who never went to college, wore leather pants all the time even though she was a vegetarian, and played bass in a weird, loud, almost all-male garage band—was the creative child, the favorite.

Yup. Dan would've gotten a kick out of that. That is, if they were still talking.

Arriving in Williamsburg, she hurried out of the subway and into the natural food store only a few blocks away. *Soy mozzarella, wheat-free lasagna noodles, tempeh . . . ,* she read from the list Ruby had given her. Tonight Ruby was making her famous soy-tempeh lasagna in honor of their parents' arrival. There was another thing that set Vanessa apart. She was a carnivore, while Ruby and her parents were all vegetarians.

She pulled a brick of tempeh out of the store's fridge. "You don't even look like food," she told it, tossing the tempeh into her shopping basket. She shook her head and smiled bitterly as she walked down the aisle in search of the wheat-free section. Her father was always talking to inanimate objects. It was part of his whole "kooky artist" mystique. But Vanessa wasn't really an artist—yet—and if she didn't find someone to talk to besides a brick of vegetarian meat replacement she didn't even like the taste of, she'd be worse than kooky: She'd just go plain insane.

"Why don't you go out and do something with your friends?" Ruby always asked whenever Vanessa looked particularly sad, bitter, and lonely. Vanessa always treated this question the same way she treated the question, Why don't you wear colors instead of only black? Because to her, black *was* a color—the *only* color. Just like Dan was her only friend. It was going to be weird when her parents asked about him, and even weirder not having anyone to hang out with over break.

Unless . . . unless she found someone to hang out with.

I appreciates a good fake fur

There he was! Jenny flew down the school steps. Leo—which was short for Leonardo, which was clearly representative of Leonardo da Vinci, who was a great, if not *the* greatest, artist in her opinion—Leo, *her* Leo, was waiting for her after school like a good boyfriend, the *best* boyfriend. Supertall and superblond, with happy blue eyes, an adorable chipped front tooth, and a loping gait. And he was hers, *all hers*!

"Look, it's your brother," she heard her new best friend, Elise Wells, say behind her as she raced toward Leo. Only a few feet away, Dan stood hunched with his hands in his pockets, as if she were ten years old again and he was waiting to pick her up.

Jenny stood on tiptoe and kissed Leo's cheek as Dan stood watching. "Hi," she murmured into Leo's ear, feeling extremely mature. With luck her entire class—no, the entire school—was watching enviously right now.

"You're all warm," Leo mumbled, taking her small hand in his awkward, gangly one. His wrist accidentally brushed her boob and he blushed.

Jenny Humphrey was tiny, the shortest girl in her ninth-grade class, but she had the biggest boobs in the entire school, or maybe the entire world. They were so big, she'd considered getting them surgically reduced, but after some consideration, she'd decided they were part of what made her *her,* and so she'd decided to keep them. And after living with them for fourteen years, she'd grown accustomed to people accidentally bumping into them because they stuck out so far, but Leo was clearly still figuring out how to deal with them.

Sure he was.

"So, what should we do?" he asked, his voice barely audible. At first, Jenny had trouble understanding him when he talked, since he spoke in near whispers and preferred e-mail to the phone. But when she thought about it, she kind of liked that no one else could possibly overhear what Leo said to her. It was like they had their own private language. And it made Leo seem more troubled and mysterious, like someone with a dark past.

Dan had heard all about Leo Berensen, the boy Jenny had met online, but he'd never met him. He walked over and introduced himself. "So you're a sophomore? At Smale? I hear graphic art is pretty big there."

"Yeah," Leo replied inaudibly, his hazel eyes barely skimming over Dan's face. Jenny hung on his arm and beamed up at him as if he'd just saved the world with his words. "Pretty much."

"Cool." Dan was kind of annoyed that he'd gone to all the trouble of meeting Jenny after school so he could brag about his *Red Letter* internship, and now this blond half-wit was in the way.

"Um, I hate to break this up, guys, but can we like, *go somewhere?*" Elise Wells begged from outside their little circle. Her stiff blond bob was tucked behind cold, pink-tinged ears. "I'm getting hypothermic."

Not at all surprising, considering that her gray pleated uniform was rolled up so high it barely covered her butt cheeks. Elise's style had always been preppy-good-girl-meets-cheap-slut, but lately she'd been erring on the cheap-slut side.

"Let's take the bus across town to my house together," Jenny chirped happily. She had never felt so . . . *sought after* in all her life. "Maybe Dad will be home. He's dying to meet you," she told Leo.

Dan smiled to himself as he followed them up Fifth Avenue to Ninety-sixth Street. More likely, their dad was going to eat Leo for lunch.

Elise walked beside him, her pink sweater sleeves pulled down over her hands to keep them warm. "So you're a real poet, huh?" she asked as the bus pulled up and they got on. Jenny and Leo were already sitting together, holding hands. Dan scooted into a seat right behind them, and Elise sat down next to him. "I hate creative writing. Our teacher acts like everyone is full of ideas all the time—we just have to write them down. But every time we have an in-class writing assignment, I can't think of anything to write. You know?"

Dan didn't know. For him in-class writing assignments were total gifts from heaven. He was so full of ideas he didn't have *time* to write them all down. Still, it was kind of refreshing to talk to someone who thought of him as a *real poet*.

"Actually, I just found out I'm going to be doing an internship at *Red Letter* during spring break. I'm pretty excited about it. I mean, those internships are pretty hard to get."

Elise cocked her head and pressed her lips together. "Red what?

"You know, *Red Letter*. It's like the most successful avant-garde literary quarterly in the world."

"Oh," Elise glanced at him sideways, like she was checking to see if he was even cuter in profile.

He kind of was, especially with those new hipster side-burns.

"Can I read some of your poetry?" she asked brazenly.

Jenny turned around when she heard this. So Elise was flirting with her brother. She glanced up at Leo and considered whispering something to him about it, but Leo wasn't really the gossiping type.

Can you spell *b-o-r-i-n-g*?

But then Leo surprised her by leaning in to whisper in her ear. "See the coat that woman across from you is wearing? It's fake, but you can tell it's J. Mendel by the color. Most fake furs are done all in one color, but real mink fur is lots of different colors. J. Mendel makes the best fakes."

Jenny stared at the woman's coat, unsure of what to make of all this. Fake fur was kind of a weird thing for a guy to know about. She hadn't asked what his parents did for a living yet. Maybe they were importers of exotic Russian furs or poachers or something.

"How—?" She turned her head to reply, but Leo was staring intently out the window as they zoomed through Central Park, so deep in thought, she didn't want to interrupt him. Gazing into the dark hollow of his left ear, she wondered if he might even be partially deaf, and hence the mumbling. He even had a little scar on his neck that might have been from chicken pox, or a gunshot.

She gripped his hand more tightly. Oh how wonderful to have a Leo, a wild and wonderfully mysterious Leo!

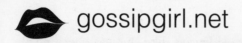 gossipgirl.net

topics ◀ previous next ▶ post a question reply

Disclaimer: All the real names of places, people, and events have been altered or abbreviated to protect the innocent. Namely, me.

hey people!

Me, glorious me

It seems that lately everyone who is anyone is talking about *me*. Totally flattering, yes, but also totally fruitless. There's no better place to go incognito than here in Manhattan, where anyone notable at least pretends not to want to be noticed. You know how celebrities like Cameron Diaz are always walking around in baseball caps and sunglasses to hide their identities? Normal people don't have to do that, so if you do it, you immediately draw attention to yourself and people constantly try to figure out who you are, which is exactly the point. Basically, I'm a glutton for this kind of attention— I *love* it! Why would I give it up by revealing who I am? Then again, if you happened to be a certain boy I happen to have an undying crush on, and you took an interest in finding out who I was, I just might kiss and tell. . . .

Your e-mail

Dear GG,

So I was wondering what you think about the idea of taking a year off instead of going to college, and following a band I like that tours a lot. I could earn some money by selling cookies or tie-dyes in the parking lot at their shows or whatever and just find out what life is about. I mean, my parents want me to go to college, but I thought it would be more fun maybe to just do my own thing, you know?

—cheese

A:

Hi cheese,

I don't know. It doesn't sound like the best-thought-out plan to me. I don't suppose you have a major crush on the lead singer of that band or anything, do you? Cuz it's not like he's going to fall in love with you, even if he sees your face in the front row at every show for a year, and especially not if you're out in the parking lot selling cookies. Also, I think college is going to be fun. A different kind of fun, but a *lot* of fun. I know guys in bands are totally sexy, but from what I've heard, every college is full of guys in bands, and you and they will all be living and *sleeping* on the same small campus. Now doesn't that sound like fun?

—GG

Sightings

N with his buddies in the park, lighting up. A myth, we think. **G**, his crazy steel-heiress girlfriend, on a rehab-nurse-accompanied trip to the **Darien Sport Shop** in Connecticut to outfit herself with cute **Bogner** ski outfits and **Rossignol**'s fastest racing skis. **C**, also in the Darien Sport Shop, with his mom, buying a new snowboard and ogling **G**. **S** and **B** in **Barneys**' sleepwear and lingerie department, stocking up on girly things to lounge around in during their extended sleepover party at **S**'s house. **D** in the literary journal section of **Coliseum Books**, cramming for his new job. **V** filming pigeons roosting outside her bedroom window. So that's what she's resorted to? And a couple of middle-aged artists who might sort of resemble **V**, if she had stringy gray hair, at the opening of their found-sculpture exhibit at the **Holly Smoke Gallery** in the Meatpacking District. One piece involved a moldy wheel of Brie cheese and an inflatable bed. We won't ask.

Only two more days left before break, and tomorrow night we've got that party. More before then.

You know you love me.

gossip girl

b gets horny just looking at his shoes

"You can sleep in here," Serena told Blair as the two girls dragged Blair's overstuffed Louis Vuitton duffel bags into Erik's room. "My brother took his TV and stereo and everything with him, so it's kind of bare in here, but we'll hang out in my room most of the time. . . ."

"That's okay," Blair said, looking around. Compared to the sumptuous décor of the rest of the van der Woodsens' apartment, the room was pretty sparse. A single antique sleigh bed stood under the double-sized windows that faced Fifth Avenue, the Met, and Central Park. Beside it was a long, low dresser, and on the opposite wall was a desk and chair, all in the same dark wood as the bed. On the floor was a woven Turkish rug in shades of navy blue and tangerine. The closet door stood partially open so that Blair could see the silhouette of Erik's old denim jacket, hanging on the rail.

Blair breathed in the room's musty wood smell. The idea of sleeping in the lair of an older boy she didn't know that well was strangely exciting. "Do you mind if I unpack my stuff?"

"Sure, go ahead." Serena flopped on the bed and pulled a

Playboy magazine out from under Erik's mattress, scrunching up her perfectly straight nose as she flipped through it.

Both girls were too savvy about what boys really do when they're in their rooms alone to squirm and scream at the sight of *Playboy*.

Blair pulled a pair of pants out of her bag and opened the closet. Beside the denim jacket, two white J. Press button-down shirts with frayed collars and cuffs hung next to a barely worn black Hugo Boss tuxedo. On the floor of the closet was a pair of beaten-up Stan Smith tennis shoes, and next to them was a Prada shoe box.

Blair glanced at Serena, but her friend was completely transfixed by *Playboy*. She knelt down, wondering what kind of person would leave their Prada shoes behind. The black box was dusty, and when she lifted the lid she found there were no shoes inside, only a small brown leather-bound notebook. Gingerly, she lifted it out and opened it up to the first page.

I can't believe I'm fucking writing in a journal like a fucking girl, but I'm drunk on tequila from Case's graduation party and instead of passing out like a normal person, I'm fucking freaking out. We just graduated. We're going to college. I don't know who I am or what I'm doing or who I want to be and now I'm leaving everything I know and FUCK! Serena is so lucky—she's only just started high school, and I'll be able to tell her what the deal is with college, so she'll know. No one's going to tell ME. And it's not like I'm going to walk up to any of my friends and admit how scared I am. All they talk about is the girls we can have sex with. And I'm sure that will happen, unless I become one of those freaks who lives in a single and never comes out of his room and they finally

have to break in because of the smell. Fuck, this is crazy.
I'm going to bed.

Blair turned the pages to read more, but the rest of the book had been left blank. Obviously, Erik had decided journal-writing wasn't for him. Her heart beat loudly as she reread the first and only entry. How crazy was it that Erik van der Woodsen, a boy she hardly knew, had captured the way she'd been feeling these last few weeks so completely perfectly?

She stood up and walked over to a silver-framed family photograph on top of Erik's dresser. The van der Woodsens were sprawled on a beach somewhere in their bathing suits, all with tanned skin, pale blond hair, white smiles, and huge dark blue eyes. Blair could tell Serena was about fourteen in the picture because she still had those bangs she'd gotten at the end of eighth grade and spent the next year growing out. So Erik must have been seventeen. In his weather-beaten blue surf shorts his body looked muscular and ready for action, but his handsome face was slightly weary, like he'd been up all night carousing, or maybe he was even a little sad.

Why didn't I ever notice before? Blair wondered to herself. Behind her Serena rustled the pages of *Playboy*.

"Does Erik have a girlfriend?" Blair wondered out loud.

"Let's ask him ourselves." Serena tossed the magazine on the floor and reached for the phone, a mischievous grin playing on her face. She was used to bothering Erik up at Brown at least three times a week, moaning to him about her love life or lack thereof, while he complained about his perma-hangover.

"Hey, perverted man. I was just reading your gross *Playboy* with the Demi Moore centerfold. Isn't she like fifty years old or something?"

"So?" Erik yawned in reply.

"So how lucky are you that Mom and Dad don't drag you around to boring benefits anymore?"

"What is it tonight?"

"Tomorrow night. Some art thing at the Frick," Serena answered tiredly. "It's not even worth getting a new dress for. Blair and I are just going to trade clothes so they feel new. Anyway, she wants to ask you something." And then, without warning, Serena tossed the phone to Blair.

Blair caught it and held it in her hands. "Hello?" she heard Erik say. She put the phone to her ear.

"Hey. It's Blair. Um, I'm staying in your room. I hope that's okay."

"Sure. Hey, listen, my sister told me a while ago you're really worried about Yale and your shitty interview and all that. . . ."

Blair's eyes widened in horror. Her fucked-up Yale interview was the last thing Erik needed to know about her. Serena was such a—

"Well, don't be," Erik continued. "My Brown interview was completely retarded, and I got in early. I know for a fact you're an ace at tennis, you do a shitload of charity stuff, and Serena says your grades and scores are all amazing. So don't sweat it, okay?"

"Okay," Blair promised tremulously. No wonder Serena called her brother all the time. He was absolutely the sexiest, sweetest boy alive!

"So, are you coming to Sun Valley with us for break or what?" he asked.

Blair kicked off her turquoise flats and wiggled her red-painted toes. She liked the matted, scratchy feeling of Erik's rug beneath her bare feet. "I'm supposed to go to Hawaii with my family."

"No, you're not," Serena interjected from the bed. "She's not!" she yelled, loud enough for Erik to hear. "She's coming to Sun Valley with us!"

"You don't really *want* to go to Hawaii, do you?" Erik asked her half-gently, half-mockingly. "You'd much rather go skiing with us."

Blair studied Erik's face in the photograph. Had he *always* talked to her in that familiar, you-know-you-want-me tone of voice? Had she always been totally *deaf?* She imagined lounging by the fire with him in the bar at the Sun Valley Lodge. She'd play Marilyn Monroe at her red-hot skinniest, dressed in a white rabbit fur vest, her favorite pair of Seven jeans, and the white sheepskin après-ski boots she'd bought in January and never worn. He'd be . . . Ernest Hemingway, all manly and studied, wearing one of those tight, navy blue zip-neck turtlenecks the sexy ski patrol guys always wore, half unzipped. They'd sip warm brandy and watch the shadows cast by the flames flickering on each other's faces, while she caressed his strong, warm muscles beneath his shirt.

Three years ago, Erik had had no idea who he was or what he was doing or who he wanted to be, but now it was three years later, and he'd definitely figured it out. Just the thought of sleeping in his bed tonight was extremely comforting. She might even wear one of his old shirts to bed for added atmosphere.

"Yes," Blair told him in her breathiest Marilyn Monroe voice. "Yes, I think I *will* go."

And you, sweet boy, are in for a special treat.

can n resist hot board chick with dope breath?

The following day, after lacrosse practice and before he had to be home to get ready for the benefit at the Frick, Nate made a detour to the Scandinavian Ski Shop on West Fifty-seventh Street to outfit himself for Sun Valley. He had been skiing and snowboarding practically since he was born and already had tons of ski equipment, but it was all up in Maine—and besides, this was the type of shopping he actually enjoyed.

The Scandinavian Ski Shop specialized in thousand-dollar fur-trimmed Bogner ski suits and fur après-ski boots for the Madison Avenue set, and had a sort of phony Tyrolean Woods feel to it, with wood-paneled walls and thick, forest green wall-to-wall carpeting, but it was still the best ski shop in New York.

Nate went right to the back of the store where the skis and snowboards were sold. He shoved his hands in his khaki pants pockets, contemplating the boards stacked against the wall. Instantly, his eyes settled on a dark red Burton board with a picture of a green pot leaf on it. The word *normal* was stenciled on one end of the board, and the word *goofy* was stenciled on the other. He reached up and ran his thumb along the edge of the board.

"That one's killer if you're into bumps," a girl's smoky voice drifted over to him.

Nate turned to find a small girl with short blond hair and a pug nose watching him. She was wearing an olive green Roxy hoodie and light gray Roxy board pants. Her brown eyes hung low in their sockets, puppy-dog-like. Or maybe she was stoned.

"Do you work here?" he asked.

The girl smiled. Her teeth were very small and close together. "Sometimes. When I'm on break. I go to Holden, up in New Hampshire? I'm captain of the girls' snowboard team." She kept on smiling a little too long, and Nate decided she was definitely high.

"Can I help you with something?" she offered.

Nate tapped his fingers against the red board. "I think I'm gonna take this one. Plus I need boots and bindings."

The girl kept smiling as she hunted around in a stack of boxes for a pair of Raichle boots in his size and the best K2 bindings on the market. "I just demoed this combo at Stowe last weekend." She knelt at Nate's feet to help him on with the boots. "It totally rocked."

Nate stood up and stared down the front of her hoodie, which was unzipped to just above her cleavage. She wasn't wearing a bra, just a white tank top, and he could see everything.

She smiled up at him, holding his booted foot in her hands. "How does that feel?"

He considered reaching for her hand and leading her into a dressing room. He could even imagine how her mouth would have the smoky, grassy taste that he liked, the after-you-smoke-fine-herb taste. It was odd, but ever since he'd quit smoking pot, he was basically horny all the time. And having a girlfriend in rehab who was only allowed *supervised* visits from outsiders didn't help much.

Georgie, Georgie, Georgie. He couldn't wait for Sun Valley. They'd ski all day and fool around all night. What could be better? "Can I get these mounted now?" he asked, in a hurry all of a sudden.

The girl gathered up the bindings and retrieved the correct-size board from the stack. "I'll mount 'em for you."

Sure she will.

"Be right back."

While he waited, Nate wandered over to a pile of ski hats and began to try them on. He picked out a fuzzy heathered green one with earflaps and a long tassel on top—very granola-meets-Ralph Lauren—and put it on.

"No way," he muttered as he examined himself in the mirror. Usually he didn't think too much about what he looked like or what he wore—he didn't have to—but he wanted to look cool for Georgie. He put the green hat back on the stack and tried on a black fleece baseball-type hat with earflaps you could flip up, kind of like a modern version of the Elmer Fudd hunting cap.

"That hat is awesome on you," the salesgirl told him, coming back with his board. She leaned the board against a clothes rack and walked over to Nate, gently turning down the earflaps over his perfect ears. "You know you love it," she added hoarsely.

Sure enough, her breath smelled just the way he'd imagined it would. Nate licked his lips. "What's your name?"

"Maggie."

Nate nodded slowly. The hat felt good on his head. He could reach for Maggie right now and unzip her top. Ask her if she wanted to share a joint. He could, he could. But he wouldn't.

He pulled the hat off and tucked it under his arm. "Thanks a lot for your help. Um, I'm Nate Archibald. My family has an account here?"

Maggie handed him the board and his new boots with a disappointed grin. "Maybe I'll bump into you out on the slopes sometime."

Nate turned to go, amazed at his willpower. He was so totally focused, even Coach might have been impressed.

Not that he wasn't still horny as hell.

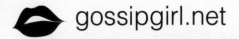 gossipgirl.net

topics ◀ *previous*   *next* ▶   *post a question*   *reply*

Disclaimer: All the real names of places, people, and events have been altered or abbreviated to protect the innocent. Namely, me.

hey people!

Virtue vs. Vice

So, is *everyone* getting dragged to that Virtue vs. Vice benefit with our parents at the Frick tonight? I hope so—at least that means I won't be alone in my misery. Of course we all know the only reason they insist on us going is so they can compare us with one another and talk about what colleges we've applied to and who's already in early and generally drive us out of our minds, since those are definitely our least favorite subjects at the moment. Plus, there couldn't be a stuffier venue for a party. I mean, come on, a party at the Frick is like a party at your grandmother's country house.

I know I sound ungrateful—come on, a party is a party, and you know how much I love to get dressed up. But I prefer to party sans parents, don't you? The only cool thing is that our parents will all be so busy trying to impress one another that they won't bother scolding us for smoking in the powder room. Actually, if we do anything even slightly embarrassing they'll just have to pretend they don't know us. So let's try to have a little fun, shall we? See? You're already looking forward to tonight, aren't you?

I'm going to save your e-mail and sightings for after the big bash.

See you there!

You know you love me.

upper west siders look down their noses at the poorly versed

"Ladies and gentlemen, please take your seats!" Rufus Humphrey bellowed as he delivered a platter of sizzling sausages with rum-roasted apples and bananas to the table. Jenny had made her dad feel so guilty for being out the day before when she'd brought Leo home that Rufus had insisted she invite Leo and Elise over for dinner the next night. Not that Rufus was out to impress his houseguests: As usual, he was wearing a food-stained white undershirt and his favorite pair of cigarette-burned, saggy-assed gray sweatpants. His curly gray hair and monstrous gray eyebrows stuck out at odd angles from his stubbly face, and his mouth and teeth were stained red from wine.

"We'd better sit down," Jenny said, clicking off the TV in the library and grinning at Leo. "Now you get to taste Dad's weird food. Be careful," she warned. "He puts alcohol in everything."

Leo looked at his watch. Then he stuck his hands in his jeans pockets and pulled them out again. He seemed nervous. "Okay."

"Her dad isn't as scary as he looks," Elise said. She tucked her feet into her pink J. Crew clogs and clomped out into the dining room, as if she'd lived at Jenny's house all her life.

Dan met them at the creaky dining room table. He was reading from a copy of *Red Letter* and didn't even look up when his dad slapped a whole banana and a maimed-looking sausage on his plate. Once everyone was served, Rufus filled his wineglass to the rim and held it in the air. "Now for a little poetry game!"

Dan and Jenny rolled their eyes at each other across the table.

Normally Jenny didn't mind her dad's little pop quizzes, games, and lectures, but with Leo there, it was just too embarrassing. "*Dad,*" she whined. Why couldn't he be normal just this once?

Rufus ignored her. "*Where are we going, Walt Whitman? / The doors close in an hour. / Which way does your beard point tonight?!*" He directed a sausage-fat-greased finger at Leo. "Name that poet!"

"*Dad!*" Jenny rattled the decaying wooden dining-room table in protest. Everything in the Humphreys' sprawling four-bedroom Ninety-ninth Street and West End Avenue apartment was decaying. But what could you expect when they had no mother and no maid to clean up after them?

"Oh, come on. That's an easy one!" Rufus roared at Leo. The vinyl record he'd put on before he brought out the food suddenly kicked in, and the strange, high-pitched Peruvian yodelings of Yma Sumac filled the room. Rufus poured himself another glass of wine, waiting expectantly for an answer.

Leo smiled politely. "Um . . . I'm not sure if I know. . . ."

Dan leaned over and whispered loudly in Leo's ear, "Allen Ginsberg. 'A Supermarket in California.' Easy."

Jenny kicked her brother's foot under the table. Did he have to be such a wiseass?

Rufus gritted his teeth. *"But I have promises to keep, / And miles to go before I sleep,"* he challenged, his muddy brown eyes bulging as they stared Leo down.

Leo's blond hair looked almost translucent as he withered under Rufus's relentless gaze. "Um . . ."

"Dad!" Jenny cried for the third time. *"God."* She knew her father was only trying to do his wild-and-wonderful-dad bit, overcompensating for six other nights that week when she and Dan had eaten takeout in front of the TV, but didn't he get the hint that poetry was not Leo's thing?

"Well, even I know that one," Elise piped up. "Robert Frost. 'Stopping by Woods on a Snowy Evening.' I had to memorize it in eighth grade." She turned to Dan. "See, I kind of do know something about poetry."

Rufus speared a bratwurst and slapped it onto Leo's cracked blue plate. "Where do you go to school, anyway?"

Leo wiped his mouth with the back of his hand. "Smale. The Smale School, sir." His eyes darted across the table to Jenny, who smiled encouragingly.

"Hmm," Rufus responded, picking up a sausage in his fingers and biting it in half. He washed the bite down with a gulp of wine. "Never heard of it."

"It specializes in the arts," Dan said.

"And poetry isn't an art?" Rufus demanded.

Jenny couldn't eat. She was too mad at her dad. Normally, he was kind of nice in a gruff and grumpy kind of way. Why did he have to go and be so mean to Leo?

"So, a job at *Red Letter*," Rufus said, raising his glass to Dan. "I still can't believe it." Rufus had a trunk full of unread, unfinished poems in his home office, and although he was an editor himself, he had never been published. Now Dan was having the writing career he'd never had.

" 'Atta boy!" he growled. "Just don't start talking in phony accents like all those other bastards."

Dan frowned, remembering Siegfried Castle's difficult-to-understand German accent. It had sounded pretty authentic to him. "What do you mean?"

Rufus chuckled as he dug into a banana. "You'll see. Anyhow, I'm proud of you, kid. You keep this up, you'll be poet laureate by the time you're twenty."

All of a sudden, Leo stood up abruptly. "Excuse me. I have to go."

"No!" Jenny jumped to her feet. She'd imagined they'd eat quickly and then Elise would leave and she and Leo would go into her room and kiss for a while and maybe do their homework together. She might even paint his portrait if he let her. "Please stay."

"Sorry, Jenny." Leo turned to Rufus and held his hand out stiffly. "It was nice to meet you, Mr. Humphrey. Thanks for the delicious dinner."

Rufus waved his fork in the air. "Don't get too used to it, son. Most of the time we eat Chinese."

That was true. Rufus's idea of grocery shopping was to buy wine, cigarettes, and toilet paper. Jenny and Dan would have been malnourished if they hadn't been able to order in.

Jenny escorted Leo to the door. "Are you okay?" she asked worriedly.

Leo grinned his shy, cracked-tooth grin and smiled down at her from his great height. "Yeah, I just thought we'd eat a little earlier. I need to get home and—" He stopped, frowning as he wound a brand-new-looking red-and-black cashmere scarf around his neck. *Burberry*, the tag on the scarf read. Jenny had never seen him wear it before. "I'll e-mail you later," he added before disappearing down the hall to catch the elevator.

Jenny went back to the table, and Rufus raised his bushy eyebrows at her bemusedly. "Was it something I said?"

Jenny glared back at him. She had no idea why Leo had left so suddenly, but blaming her dad was the easiest solution.

"Oh, come on, Jen," her father continued heartlessly. "So he's not the sharpest tool in the box. He'll probably make a good boyfriend, though."

She stood up. "I'm going to my room."

"Do you want me to come?" Elise offered.

Jenny thought Elise looked pretty happy sitting next to Dan and talking about poetry. She'd even helped herself to a glass of wine. "No, that's okay," she mumbled. All she really wanted was lie facedown on her bed and ruminate over Leo, alone.

Elise took a sip of her wine. "I should go in a minute, anyway." She glanced sideways at Dan while still looking at Jenny, as if to say, *So, guess what? I really like your brother.* "I'm thinking of writing a poem when I get home."

Yeah, right . . .

When she got to her room, Jenny stretched out on her single bed and stared sullenly across the room at her paints and empty easel. She was positive Leo wasn't dumb, even though that Robert Frost poem was pretty well known. Actually, he was probably a lot smarter than the rest of them, just in less obvious ways. She remembered the first time she'd laid eyes on him in Bendel's before they'd met on the Internet. It was in the cosmetics department, and he was poking through the Bendel's signature brown-and-white-striped cosmetics bags, the only male shopper in the whole store. What had he been doing there, anyway? It was a mystery. And what about that random observation he'd made yesterday about that woman in the fake mink coat? Or his new Burberry scarf? He seemed to know a lot about . . . *nice things*. And why hadn't he invited her home yet? His house was probably gorgeous. And he'd never once even mentioned his parents. The mysteries of Leo just kept piling up.

And there's nothing a girl likes better than decoding the secrets of a mysterious guy.

one artist's idea of funny is another artist's idea of dumb

The second night of their visit, Vanessa's parents took her and Ruby to the gallery where their found-art sculpture exhibit was showing.

The gallery was huge and bright, with pale wood floors and white walls. In the middle of the largest room stood a brown-and-white shire horse, happily devouring a supersized Caesar salad out of an enormous wooden bowl. Beside the horse was a blue plastic bucket with a pitchfork sticking out of it. Whenever the horse pooped, the stylish German girl behind the desk near the door of the gallery would jump out of her swivel chair to shovel it up with the pitchfork and dump it in the bucket.

Vanessa's twenty-two-year-old sister Ruby stroked the horse's nose and fed him peppermint Tic Tacs, the gallery lights bouncing off her purple leather pants.

"That's Buster. He's sweet, isn't he?" their mother, Gabriela, asked, admiring the horse. "We found him eating romaine in our community garden. His owner was an angel to let us borrow him." She pulled her long gray braid over her shoulder and stroked the end of it. The garish African caftan she'd chosen to wear that evening hung from her broad shoulders like a purple, yellow, and green tablecloth with a hole cut in the top for her head. Shunning fashion altogether, Gabriela preferred "tribal costumes" and liked to think of herself as a "global fashion model." She was even wearing Mexican moccasins made from the hides of wild pigs.

Buster *was* sweet, but what made him *art*? Vanessa wondered. She went over to something nailed to the wall, only to discover that it was a chain of metal cheese graters. Some of them even had dried bits of orange cheese stuck to them.

"You're probably thinking, 'I could have made that,' " her father, Arlo Abrams, observed.

"Not really," Vanessa replied. Why the hell would she want to make a chain of cheese graters?

Arlo shuffled over to her wearing a dusty black wool Peruvian cape, an ankle-length hemp skirt—yes, that's right, a skirt—and white canvas tennis shoes. Gabriela was responsible for dressing him, otherwise he wouldn't have bothered with clothes at all. His long gray hair fanned out around his shoulders, and, as usual, he looked gaunt and alarmed. Vanessa was pretty sure the alarmed part was from all the acid he'd taken when he was younger. And who knew, maybe he was still taking it.

"Close your eyes and run your hands over them," Arlo instructed, reaching for Vanessa's hand. His breath smelled like the barbecued tempeh Ruby had put in the lasagna last night, or maybe she was smelling the old cheese on the graters.

Vanessa closed her eyes, wondering if this was the moment when she would come to understand the brilliance and purpose of her parents' work. She allowed her father to run her fingers over the pointy, sharp nubs of the graters. It felt exactly like touching cheese graters, nothing more and nothing less. She opened her eyes.

"Creepy, huh?" was all Arlo said, his hazel eyes twitching.

Creepy was right.

Across the room, Ruby and Gabriela were standing over a pot of dirt—another one of their found artworks—giggling like ten-year-olds.

"What's so funny?" Vanessa asked, thinking they were probably talking about one of Ruby's weird musician boyfriends or something. Then she noticed that even the snooty blond German girl behind the desk had cracked a smile. "What?" Vanessa repeated.

Arlo chuckled and ran his paint-stained fingers through his long gray hair, looking incredibly pleased with himself. "There are seeds in that dirt," he whispered, his eyes popping. "You know, *seeds*!"

Huh?

Vanessa had always been a loner at school, with her shaved head and her penchant for wearing only black, but usually her solitude was voluntary. In this case she *wanted* to get the joke, she really did. But she just *didn't*. And if her parents thought art was a horse eating salad or some kitchen utensils tacked to a wall or a pot of dirt with seeds in it, there was just no way they'd ever understand the dark intensity of her morbid, subtle films. And there was no way she was ever going to share her films with them.

"Ready to skedaddle?" Gabriela called over from the pot of dirt. The family's hippie art-school friends, the Rosenfelds, had invited them to some sort of art benefit, and they'd decided to drag Vanessa and Ruby along.

"Where are we going, anyway?" Vanessa asked skeptically as they stood outside the gallery, waiting for a cab. She imagined spending the rest of the evening dancing barefoot around a fire in some sculpture park in Queens to beckon the spirits of spring or some equally lame hippie nonsense.

"Somewhere called the Frick. It's on Fifth Street, I think." Gabriela started to dig around in her shapeless purse, which a friend had constructed for her out of recycled tractor tires. "I've got the address written down somewhere."

"It's Fifth *Avenue*," Vanessa corrected. "I know where it is." And she was pretty sure there weren't going to be a whole lot of men in skirts there, either.

No, but it would be a lot more fun if there were.

freak-out at the frick

The Frick had been the New York residence of Henry Clay Frick, the industrial-era coke and steel magnate. Mr. Frick was a great collector of European art, and after he died, the mansion was turned into a museum.

The Virtue vs. Vice benefit was in the Living Hall, a large, oak-paneled room laid with a Persian carpet and displaying paintings by major sixteenth-century artists such as El Greco, Holbein, and Titian. At the middle of one wall stood one of Soldani's bronze sculptures, *Virtue Triumphant over Vice,* and in the center of each of the huge round tables set for the party with cream-colored linens and sparkling silver stood a ten-inch-high replica of the same sculpture, surrounded by a garland of purple tulips.

Not that anyone was paying any attention to the art.

Women in custom-made couture gowns and men in tuxedos milled around the tables or stood by the bar, nibbling plum-dipped duck fritters and talking about everything *except* art.

"Did you see the van der Woodsen girl in that new perfume advertisement?" Titi Coates murmured to Misty Bass.

"The phony tear was just too much. I thought it was rather exploitative, didn't you?" Misty declared. She nodded pointedly as Serena and Blair followed Serena's parents into the room before the two girls veered off to find something to drink.

"Your boobs must stick out further than mine." Serena hiked up the black strapless Donna Karan dress she'd borrowed from Blair. They wore the same size bra, so she'd thought the dress would stay up fine, but every time she took a step, she could feel the dress inching floorward.

"Yeah, but you're skinnier." Blair wasn't about to admit it, but Serena's pink Milly cocktail dress had been gradually ripping under her arms and in the seams in the bodice ever since she zipped it up. Every so often she'd hear another little *rip* as the threads gave way, but hopefully the dress would hold up until they got home.

Everyone seemed to be drinking cocktails, but the cocktail servers were nowhere to be found. "Why are we here again?" Blair whined.

"I don't know. It's just one of those things," Serena answered contritely.

"Well, if they don't have Ketel One vodka this year, I'm leaving," Blair grumbled. Last year she'd had to settle for Absolut, which was so passé, it was practically prehistoric.

"Isn't it wonderful to see those two girls together again?" Blair's mother breathed in Mrs. van der Woodsen's ear. "It was no good when Serena was away at boarding school. We girls need to keep our friends close."

"Yes, quite," Mrs. van der Woodsen agreed coolly as she averted her blue eyes from Eleanor's pregnant belly. She and Eleanor had always been friendly, but a baby at nearly fifty was simply too vulgar. And that fat, loud, mustachioed real estate developer she was married to was a little hard to take. "Oh, look, there's Misty Bass. Let's go and say hello."

Misty had left Titi Coates arguing with her daughter, Isabel, about whether Isabel should get a car for graduation or not, and now Misty was sitting alone with her son, Chuck, gossiping as usual. She was a severe blond in a gold Carolina Herrera gown and vintage Harry Winston jewels, and he was a dark, deceptively handsome devil in a gray Prada zoot suit with green pinstripes.

In fact, Chuck really *was* the devil, and he was always looking for new ways to express his evil. But be patient, we'll get to that.

"Pushing fifty and nearly seven months along," Misty whispered to her son. "What does your friend Blair make of it?"

Chuck shrugged as if he could have cared less. At Serena's big New Year's Eve bash, he'd sidled up to Blair and proposed that she give up her virginity to him, since he was rather an expert at deflowering. To his irritation, Blair had flatly refused. Lately he'd been experimenting with being gay, if only to stave off boredom.

Or to have an excuse to wax his eyebrows.

"She probably made herself puke a few extra times," Chuck observed callously, referring to Blair's little bulimia problem, which was hardly a secret. "She'll be out of the house soon after the kid's born, anyway."

"I heard Blair's going to a clinic right after graduation to take care of her problem once and for all," Misty Bass noted. "Isn't that right?"

But Chuck had stopped listening. Across the room a little drama was unfolding, and he didn't want to miss it.

Nate hadn't even laid eyes on Blair since she'd stalked him all the way to rehab in Greenwich, Connecticut, a few weeks ago. During her one and only appearance in group therapy, the counselor had forced her to admit out loud in front of the group that she was bulimic, although Blair had insisted on calling it "stress-induced regurgitation." Nate might have been amused by Blair's dramatic appearance at the clinic, but at the time he was just beginning to hook up with Georgie, and two crazy girls at once were simply too much for him to handle. Thankfully, Blair saw right away that her plan of attack had backfired and promptly decided that rehab was beneath her.

As if she really wanted to spend Saturday afternoons talking about how she occasionally stuck her finger down her throat instead of shopping for shoes with Serena. No, thank you.

And what about Serena? Nate couldn't even remember the last time he'd seen her, but as always she looked glamorous and poised, in that charming, understated way of hers. Usually Nate liked to hang out in one place at parties and let people come to him if they felt like talking, but he decided to go over and say hello. Why the hell not? Even if Blair wouldn't speak to him, Serena would.

Serena was the first to see him coming. She flicked her cigarette, ashing on the mansion's priceless marble floor. "Nathaniel Archibald," she declared, partly to warn Blair, but partly out of pleased surprise. "Our long-lost Nate."

"Fucking hell." Blair stamped out her Merit Ultra Light with the pointy heel of one of her black satin Manolo Blahnik party shoes. "Jesus."

Serena wasn't sure if Blair was swearing because Nate was the last person on earth she wanted to see or because Nate looked so devastatingly hot in his classic Armani tux.

There's nothing more breathtaking than a delicious boy in a tuxedo, even if you're supposed to be hating him.

"Hey." Nate kissed Serena quickly on the cheek and then tucked his hands into his tuxedo jacket pockets, smiling cautiously at Blair. She was twirling her ruby ring around and around on her little finger like she always did when she was nervous. Her short haircut made her cheekbones stand out more, or maybe she'd lost some weight. Anyway, she looked sort of . . . fierce. Fierce and delicate at the same time. "Hey, Blair."

Blair dug her fingernails into her palm. She needed another drink. "Hello. How's rehab?"

"Over. At least for me. That girl I'm seeing—Georgie—she's still there."

"Because she's a drug addict?" Blair responded, tossing back the last of her vodka.

The boisterous big-band music that no one had even noticed was playing suddenly stopped, chilling the room.

"We're getting drunk," Serena cut in before Blair could do anything insane, like karate-chop Nate's head off. "Only one more day of school left before break!"

Nate flagged down a passing waiter and got them all more vodka. "You guys going anywhere good?"

"Sun Valley—just like always," Serena told him.

Blair just stood there guzzling her second drink and wishing a) that Nate would go away, b) that he didn't look quite so dashing and nonstoned, c) that he would stop being so absurdly friendly, and d) that Serena would stop being so friendly back.

"Blair's coming with us. She just got her ticket."

Nate pulled a pack of Marlboros out of his pocket and stuck one between his lips. He lit it carefully, glancing at Blair through the flame and then away again.

"Looks like I'm going there, too," he said finally. "Georgie's mom has a house near the mountain. We should ski together."

Blair felt her stomach begin to gurgle and splosh in Serena's too-tight dress.

"I'll be right back." She shoved her empty glass at Serena. "Maybe you should find our table so we can sit down."

"Blair's living at my house for a while," Serena explained to Nate as they watched Blair make a beeline for the ladies' room. All of a sudden, Serena felt sort of big-sisterly and protective toward Blair, and she was glad she'd been able to help. "Her mom's turning her room into a nursery for her new baby sister. Bummer, huh?"

Nate tried to imagine what Blair's life must be like now that she had a new stepfather and stepbrother and a new baby sister on the way. He didn't get very far.

"You look different," Serena noted, looking him up and down. She cocked a perfectly groomed eyebrow and grinned. "You look *good*."

Nate and Serena had always lusted after each other. They'd even given in and had sex once, losing their virginity together the summer before tenth grade, just before Serena had gone off to boarding school. It was a recreational sort of lust, though, with no strings attached, and they'd never acted on it again since that one time.

"I *feel* good," Nate admitted. He thought about telling her how he'd quit getting high but still hadn't made lax captain. How he couldn't wait for her to meet Georgie because they'd definitely get along. But Nate wasn't much of a gusher. "It's cool you're going out there," he said simply. "It should be a good time."

"*Should* be a good time?" Serena repeated, throwing her arms around him in her usual spontaneous manner and getting pink lip gloss all over his cheek. "Normally I only have my boring old brother to ski with. It's gonna rock!"

Nate endured the hug, trying not to get turned on. But now that he was pot-free, the mere whiff of a girl's perfume or the brush of her hand was enough to make his cheeks flush, especially when she was as gorgeous as Serena was.

Serena lifted a cigarette from out of the pack in his breast pocket and squeezed past him. "I better go check on Blair. See you later, okay?"

Nate watched her go, feeling for his cell phone in his tuxedo pants pocket. Georgie was probably in her room at Breakaway right now, having quiet time, or whatever it was they made their patients do after dinner, but maybe the nurse on duty would be nice enough to let them have phone sex.

He dialed the number and put the phone to his ear before looking up. Chuck Bass was staring at him from his seat next to his jewel-encrusted mom, looking extremely gay indeed. And just the thought that Chuck might possibly have a crush on him was enough to quell the urgency of Nate's call to Connecticut. He tucked the phone back into his pocket and went off to find his table, not even bothering to think about the rumors Chuck had already started circulating about him and Serena.

virtue vs. vice

Vanessa knew it had been a mistake to come the minute she laid eyes on Misty Bass's gold dress. Never mind the fact that her dad was wearing a wool poncho and a skirt—she was still wearing her school uniform!

But her parents didn't seem at all self-conscious. "Look at Dad checking out the free booze," Ruby whispered in her ear. "He's in freaking *heaven*."

"They need to turn the music up so people can dance," their mother commented, snapping her fingers and bobbing up and down in her moccasins. She was probably the only woman in the building not in heels—even Vanessa and Ruby were wearing platform boots.

A hushed, horrified murmur slithered through the room.

"Who the hell are *they*?" Chuck Bass asked his mom. Misty Bass was one of the grandes dames of New York Society. She knew everyone.

"I'm not sure," his mother answered. "But I do love a man in a skirt. It takes such courage!"

"You know, I recognize those two," Titi Coates told her husband. "They're the artists from the opening we went to last night—the one with that wonderful horse!"

"Gabby! Arlo!"

A woman in an elegant black floor-length gown, her high-lighted brown hair pulled back in a stylish, professionally done 'do, was waving energetically at the Abramses from a table in the corner.

"I think that must be Mrs. Rosenfeld," Vanessa dragged her parents over to the gesticulating woman.

Mwa! Mwa!

"We are just *too* glad you're here!" Pilar Rosenfeld cried, kissing each one of the Abramses twice on each cheek. "Isn't it wonderful, Roy?" she asked, touching her husband's crisp, tuxe-doed arm. "Here we all are together again after all these years."

"Splendid!" Roy Rosenfeld said in his deep, dapper voice. The Rosenfelds had gone to art school with the Abramses and had once worn only tie-dyes, cutoffs, and no shoes, even though they were both from wealthy New England families. Obviously their shoeless days had been just a phase.

Next to Mr. Rosenfeld, a tall, dark-haired boy wearing wire-rimmed Armani glasses stood peering down his formidable nose at Vanessa, as if trying to place her.

"Jordy, you remember Gabriela and Arlo and Ruby and Vanessa?" his mother asked.

The boy's haughty stance didn't change. "I think the last time I saw you, you were only a baby, but I'm pretty sure you had more hair."

Vanessa had just noticed Serena van der Woodsen and Blair Waldorf basking in their glory at the next table, making her even more aware of the fact that she was wearing her school uniform. "Last time I saw you, you were wearing tie-dyed diapers."

Jordy pushed his glasses up on the bridge of his tremen-dous nose. "Well, now I'm prelaw, at Columbia."

Ruby sat down at the table and poured herself a huge glass of champagne. "Mom? Dad? Are you guys okay?"

Their parents were standing stiffly together, propping each other up like one of their found-art statues. Vanessa wondered if they'd expected to be dancing barefoot around a fire to welcome the coming of spring instead of sitting down at a black-tie affair.

"Please." Mr. Rosenfeld pulled out the empty chair next to him and gestured for Vanessa's mother to sit down.

"I just love your skirt," Mrs. Rosenfeld noted, pointing to Arlo's accidental fashion statement. "Is that Galliano by any chance?"

Arlo stared at her blankly. A white-jacketed waiter arrived to serve the first course, a duck paté terrine. Arlo began to poke at it with his dessert spoon, checking it for signs of life. Vanessa's mother picked up her cloth napkin and blew her nose into it. Ruby snorted and giggled into her champagne.

"Are you still making art for peace, or have you given all that up?" Gabriela asked Pilar.

Pilar smiled. "Roy and I are in real estate law. Jordy wants to get into law, too, when he's done with school. Forget about it—we don't even have time to recycle anymore!"

Vanessa's parents both blanched. Recycling was what found art was all about. Without recycling, they and their art would cease to exist. "Well, that's a pity," Gabriela said, frowning down at her paté. "You don't suppose I could ask them to make us a salad, do you?"

Vanessa dug into her paté, delighted with this entertaining turn of events.

"What kind of law do you want to practice?" she asked Jordy.

He waved cigarette smoke away from his weirdly long

nostrils. Behind him, Blair Waldorf and Serena van der Woodsen were smoking like chimneys while Blair's pregnant mother polished off the food on their plates. "Probably real estate, just like my parents."

Vanessa nodded. It was sort of hard to relate someone's desire to emulate his parents when her own parents were such freaks. But Jordy's lack of imagination was also strangely appealing. And he wasn't bad-looking either, with nice wavy black hair that looked like he probably spent a lot of time grooming it, and that nose. Vanessa wouldn't have minded getting Jordy's nose on film. "I like your glasses," she told him.

Just because she had a shaved head didn't mean she didn't know how to flirt.

"Thanks." He pulled them off and then put them back on again. "You're a senior, right? Know where you're going to college next year?"

Vanessa glared at Ruby, daring her to blurt out the information about Vanessa's early acceptance at NYU. But Ruby remained loyally silent, which was a major challenge for a motormouth like her.

"What does it matter?" Arlo demanded grumpily. "Any school that can help her discover something she's passionate about would be fine."

Gabriela tugged on her long gray braid, her brown eyes passing over Vanessa absentmindedly. "That's right, you *are* going to college next year." She turned to Pilar. "Arlo always hoped Vanessa would go to Oberlin. I don't know where he got that idea. After all, it's an *arts* school."

"I'm sure some school will be dumb enough to take me," Vanessa said quietly.

"That's the spirit, dear!" Pilar chirped. "And all this time, you two girls have been living on your own in Williamsburg," she added, changing the subject. "My, you're independent!"

"Ruby's got to keep up with her music," Gabriela gushed. "Her band might get signed to a label soon."

Vanessa smiled tightly. "While I just sit around the house all day, eating meat-flavored Pringles and watching violent TV."

Next to her Jordy grunted, the only one at the table who'd gotten the joke.

The band began to play, a little louder this time. Duke Ellington, or something of that ilk. Chuck Bass shimmied over to Serena and Blair's table, his hands on his hips for added gayness. "This party would be so much less boring if you girls would dance with me." He leaned over the backs of their chairs and breathed down their bare necks.

Serena and Blair glanced at each other sideways. Their only surefire escape was to sprint to the ladies' room for more cigarettes. Grabbing their drinks, they scooted their chairs back and leapt to their feet.

Rrrrüppp!

Whoosh!

Oops!

Blair's borrowed too-tight pink dress ripped obscenely down both sides, revealing the fact that she was wearing only a pair of sheer black stockings underneath and absolutely no underwear. Worse still, Serena's strapless dress got caught on the back of her chair and was yanked down to her waist, revealing her completely bare 34Bs.

"It's all right, we're all girls here," Chuck tittered.

"Close your eyes, dear," Titi Coates snapped at her husband, Arthur.

"Oh, my!" Mrs. van der Woodsen exclaimed, reflexively reaching for her drink.

"Whoa," Nate breathed, suddenly glad he wasn't high.

The girls giggled hysterically, frantically clutching themselves and each other as they tore past Chuck, dashed to the coatroom to fetch their coats, and beat it out of the Frick as fast as their three-and-a-half-inch heels would allow.

No one at Vanessa's table had even noticed. The elder Rosenfelds and Abramses were too busy being offended by each other as the band struck up the Irving Berlin song "Puttin' on the Ritz."

Vanessa hated to dance, but she grabbed the sleeve of Jordy's expensive suit jacket, anyway. "I love this song. Come and dance with me?"

Jordy stood up and pulled back her chair for her, all manners and conformity. Then he led her onto the dance floor and twirled her around with the confident ease of someone who'd been to dancing school.

Vanessa surprised herself by feeling a little giddy as she was spun and dipped. He was such a good dancer, she completely forgot about her stupid school uniform.

Even though most of the other girls in the room would never forget.

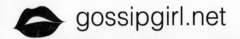 gossipgirl.net

Disclaimer: All the real names of places, people, and events have been altered or abbreviated to protect the innocent. Namely, me.

hey people!

That so-called boring, pointless party we all had to go to

Wasn't it so much better than you expected? Just think, there are only a few more hours left until spring break—and now we all have something to talk about on the airplane!

Not that I won't be talking about the thing I *never* get tired of talking about. . . .

Sex

Sure, some of us have had it and some of us haven't, but the truth is, we're all thinking about it and we're definitely all talking about it. There's the who-do-you-think-has-already-done-it-in-our-grade-and-with-whom breakdown, which always involves one girl getting accused of doing it with a teacher in sixth grade. A total lie by the way, because I happen to have been that girl. Then there's the who-would-you-do-it-with-if-you-could-do-it-with-anyone quiz, which usually involves a celebrity like Jake Gyllenhaal. Then there's the penis debate, which usually morphs into a shrieking, giggling fit, because face it, penises are ugly and weird. Then there's the my-ideal-first-time fantasy, which also usually involves celebrities. For some reason, my ideal-first-time fantasy was always with Jake, on top of a washing machine, at sunrise (our laundry room happens to have a great view of the sunrise over the East River). But then I realized how completely uncomfortable that would be—and how awkward if the maid needed to do the laundry! Needless to say, we can't *stop* talking about sex. And now that I've spilled my guts, I herewith give you permission to spill yours. Don't be shy. After all, it's totally anonymous.

Unless you don't want it to be.

Your e-mail

Q: Hey G,

So last night I was at that party and I'm pretty sure I saw you. There was this weird family that I've never seen before. The dad was wearing sneakers and like, a wraparound skirt. Do you shave your head?

—xstream

A: Dear xstream,

Your sleuthing abilities are admirable but way inaccurate. Even if I did shave my head, might I not wear a wig or a funky hat every once in a while, especially for a fancy-dress occasion like last night's party? And as I recall, the only girl in the room with a shaved head last night was also wearing her school uniform, which I must loudly insist I would never, *ever* do.

—GG

Q: dear gossipgurl,

so did you see S and N practically, like, doing it in the corner of the room at the Frick last night? they r so far in denial it's crazy. like why don't they just admit they want to be together? they would make a great couple, right?

—spec.tater

A: Dear spec.tater,

Methinks you err on the side of exaggeration. S and N are friends. Are friends not allowed to touch each other? Although it's hard not to believe they don't enjoy it a little more than they should . . .

—GG

Sightings

S and **B** streaking—literally—out of the **Virtue vs. Vice** benefit last night before dessert was even served. Personally I think **B** planned the whole thing and wired their dresses so she could escape being in the same room with **N** when he was looking so dashing. **V** skipping out of the party with that boy with the unusual nose to share intimate cappuccinos at the **Three Guys Coffee Shop** a few blocks away. True love? Was she just trying to get rid of her parents? Or both? And **J**'s new blond boyfriend, **L**—yes, we are quite sure it was him—arriving late to the **Frick**, all dolled up in a gorgeous tux, with **Madame T**, the renowned arts benefactress, on his arm. He was also seen on the Upper West Side last night, so perhaps it was just another cute blond boy. There seems to be a bounty of them in these parts.

Have a kick-ass vacation, and try not to break anything or lose anything I wouldn't break or lose! Wink, wink.

You know you love me.

gossip girl

snow white and the dutch olympic snowboarding team

"The last time I was here, our house was definitely on this road," Georgie insisted stubbornly. "But you don't know my mom. She would totally move the house somewhere else just to spite me."

Nate looked out the Sun Valley taxi window at the stunning log cabin mansions on Wood River Drive in Ketchum, Idaho, the main town in Sun Valley. Behind them rose the snow-covered mass of Mount Baldy, its robust sides alternating between pristinely groomed ski runs and swatches of dense conifer forest. Squinting, Nate could just make out the antlike trickle of skiers zigzagging down the slopes. His new board was tucked snugly in the back of the minivan in its padded red Burton case, and he couldn't wait to try it out.

"Maybe you could call and ask exactly where it is," the driver suggested, glancing at Georgie in the rearview mirror. The ride from the airport to her house was only supposed to take about twenty minutes, but they'd been driving around Sun Valley for forty-five.

"Just keep driving," Georgie commanded as she rested her head heavily against Nate's shoulder. The sleeping pill she'd mooched off the old man sitting next to her on the plane still hadn't worn off, and as usual she wasn't making any sense. Also, she was wearing purple satin Miu Miu sandals and a flimsy black halter top, which was kind of strange, considering the fact that they were going skiing. Still, her smooth, pale arms felt good in Nate's hands, and her thick, dark brown hair was so sleek and luxurious, he didn't mind. It was nice just being together in person instead of on the phone.

"Do you remember how many floors it has?" he asked, trying to be helpful. "Or if there's like, a stream next to it or something?"

"Not really," Georgie yawned. "I remember one time when we were here for Christmas, Nanny and I built a snowman together. I stole one of my mother's Fendi purses for it to carry on its stick arm."

Very helpful.

The driver was sort of creeping along the road back toward town. He seemed to have given up.

"Wait a minute," Georgie cried, sitting up.

The car jolted to a halt.

"That's it!" She grappled with the door handle and slid the minivan door open, completely unmindful of the fact that she was getting out in the middle of the road on a blind turn. "Come on!" she called to Nate impatiently. Obviously she expected the driver or the house staff to deal with the luggage.

Don't we all?

Nate had admired the sprawling timber ranch house the two other times they'd driven by it, wondering who lived there and if they were famous or something, since there were seven matching black Mercedes SUVs parked outside.

"Whose cars are these?" he asked as he followed Georgie down the snow-dusted driveway to the imposing eight-foot-high brushed-steel front doors of the house.

Georgie bit her bloodred lower lip with eager anticipation. She didn't even seem to notice that her satin sandals were already completely ruined. "I guess someone knew we were coming." The massive doors swung open with barely a nudge. "Mom doesn't believe in locks," Georgie explained. "She likes her friends to feel welcome even if she's not here."

"She's not here?" Nate had sort of assumed when Georgie first told him about the trip that they'd be hanging out with Georgie's mom—that they'd help her cook dinner and then watch movies together until her mom fell asleep on the sofa and they could sneak upstairs to have sex.

"Nah. She's in the Dominican Republic or Venezuela or somewhere. She always goes south in the winter."

They were inside the lofty foyer of the house now. The floor was made of red clay tiles. Big exposed wooden beams crisscrossed overhead. The foyer opened onto a huge sunken living room with an entire wall made of glass facing the mountains. Off the living room was a wooden deck, where steam from a hot tub rose into the air, barely masking the seven heads of the people sitting in it.

"Ooh, the hot tub's turned on!" Georgie squealed, kicking off her sandals. "Last one in has to bring the drinks!"

Nate let her run on ahead as he gazed up the wide plank staircase to the second floor. Clothes littered the stairs, and along the windowsill on the landing above were the small round skulls of wildcats.

He crossed the living room, sunlight pouring through the wall of glass and drenching his face. In front of the great stone fireplace was a grizzly bear rug.

We should be fooling around on that rug right now, he thought bitterly, but instead he had to go out and talk to a bunch of strangers in Georgie's mom's hot tub.

There were seven of them altogether, which sort of explained the seven cars, although if they were comfortable enough to sit in the hot tub together, then couldn't they just share one SUV? Georgie was already in the tub, wedged between a grinning blond guy and Chuck Bass. And they were all naked.

"Georgina told me she had a special someone," Chuck said, leering at Nate. His chest was covered with thick, dark hair. "But she didn't tell me it was the infamous Nathaniel Archibald!"

Nate sat down on the wooden bench skirting the railing of the deck. He didn't feel like getting wet or naked, not in front of all these guys.

"And this is the Dutch Olympic snowboarding team!" Georgie said, sweeping her snow-white arm in the direction of the seven blond guys dozing lazily in the hot water. "Chuck met them on the half-pipe just before the lifts closed."

"That's Jan, that's Franz, that's Josef, Conrad, Sneezy, Dopey, and Gan! Aren't they too yummy?" Chuck asked, sliding down into the tub until only his nose and eyes were out of the water. Then he popped up again. "And I'm Snow White!"

"No, *I'm* Snow White," Georgie insisted.

"Nice to meet you." Nate said, barely hiding his annoyance. If Georgie was already naked in the hot tub with the Dutch Olympic snowboarding team, then where did that leave him? A few of them could've been gay, since they were hanging out with Chuck, but they couldn't *all* be gay.

"Hey!" Georgie cried, splashing water in Chuck's face. "Quit pinching my tits!" She smiled sweetly up at Nate. "Chuck's and my mom's sisters are cousins. Or something like that," she explained. "We lost our virginity together in sixth grade."

Nate tucked his hands into his coat pockets. There wasn't

much you could say to that, but it made him realize how very little he actually knew about Georgie. She was definitely full of surprises, and most of the time they weren't good ones.

All of a sudden, Georgie splashed out of the water and streaked into the house. "I'm getting us some champagne! And if you're not in when I get back, Nate, I'm going to freaking push you in!"

But Nate had no intention of getting in. Instead, he stood up and followed her wet footprints into the kitchen. Georgie was rummaging through cases of champagne in the walk-in pantry. Her white, naked ass caved in at the sides because she was so skinny, but other than that she was perfect.

"I'm going upstairs to unpack." Nate announced, giving Georgie the opportunity to come with him so he could take *his* clothes off, in private.

"Suit yourself," Georgie replied, scooting by him with a magnum of champagne under each arm.

Upstairs Nate discovered his clothes had already been folded and put away in a cedar closet in one of the guest bedrooms. So instead of unpacking, he did a quick sweep of the bathrooms to get rid of all the random bottles of pills and anything else Georgie might try to ingest just for fun. If her mom really wasn't around, it was his responsibility to make sure she didn't drink a bottle of Nyquil and set the house on fire or something.

Once he was finished Georgie-proofing the bathrooms, he was definitely going to call Serena and Blair at the lodge. Because if he and Georgie weren't going to have a romantic week together, skiing and having sex, and she was going to be all crazy all the time, then he'd rather have a little company.

And who better to help entertain his hyperactively insane, drug-addicted girlfriend than the über-girl he'd always lusted after and his vicious-but-still-beautiful ex-girlfriend?

b takes an interest in skiing

Once they finally made it to the Sun Valley Lodge, Blair lay on her bed in their room, staring outside at the bare-branched trees and the snow, wondering if she shouldn't have gone to Hawaii after all. At least she could've gotten a tan.

"Knock, knock!" Serena yelled at the door to the room next door. "Housekeeping!"

She squealed excitedly as her long-lost brother opened the door and they embraced. Erik was all sweaty from the sauna, but he was still her big, adorable oaf. Her honey-bear.

"Hold on. I'll go change," Blair heard him say.

"Blair doesn't care what you're wearing," Serena replied. "Come and say hello." Then Blair heard the sound of bare feet padding across the carpet.

"Hey."

She raised herself up on her elbows and blinked. Erik was naked except for a white spa towel wrapped around his waist. His blond hair was wet and fell to the nape of his neck. There was a little scar on his chin where he'd fallen on the playground at the age of nine. Other than that, he was flawless.

Blair had already fallen for him after reading his diary and sleeping in his shirts. She'd never imagined the effect that seeing him in person would have on her. His huge blue eyes! His sad, sexy mouth! His perfect chest! Even his feet were perfect.

All of a sudden, she whirred into motion, sitting up and crossing her legs and ruffling her hair and looking calculatedly bored. "Hey." She stretched her arms overhead and arched her back. "So, have you been skiing yet?" she yawned.

Erik grinned. He was used to the effect he had on girls, and it was kind of cute to see his little sister's friend all grown up and sticking her chest out at him. Actually, he hadn't seen Blair since Serena had gone to boarding school and he'd left for college over two years ago. She'd always been pretty, but with her cute pixie haircut, nicely proportioned little body, and the upward tilt of her aristocratic chin, she'd developed into a genuine hottie.

"Snow's awesome right now, and it's been, like, snowing at night and then sixty degrees in the sun during the day, so you can, like, ski in shorts. Some girls are even skiing in bikini tops. And this place is serious about maintenance, too."

Blair nodded in pretend fascination. She'd skied all her life, but she liked to take it nice and easy and never embarrassed herself by wiping out. She'd brought her favorite Eres bikini for the hot tub, but from what Erik told her, she could even wear it on the slopes! Serena had warned her that he was a superfast bump skier, but maybe if she asked supernicely, he'd consider taking a little break from the bumps. They'd make a perfect couple, her in her bikini and him in his surf shorts, winding their way gracefully down the mountain to the envy of all.

"Do you think you could take me around tomorrow?" she asked. "I've only skied here once before."

Erik grinned. "Sure."

Their hotel room was large and old-fashioned, with heavy

beige velveteen drapes, oak dressers and nightstands, and a walk-in closet. But it also had all the modern amenities: CD and DVD player, Internet access, and a minibar, which Serena had just discovered. Sitting on the floor in front of the open fridge, she stuffed a complimentary Godiva truffle into her mouth and washed it down with a sip of champagne. Was Blair flirting with Erik? And was Erik actually flirting back? Weird.

"Don't mind me," she muttered under her breath as she took another swig out of the minibottle of Veuve Clicquot. "Look, the light is blinking on the phone. We have messages!" She scooted over to the bedside phone and picked up the handset, following the instructions to retrieve their voicemail.

"Hey, it's Nate. Hope you guys made it out okay. Want to meet up tomorrow morning around ten-thirty to ski? Let me know if you're up for it. Um, I don't know what the number here is. It's kind of a crazy place, actually. But call my cell. Okay. See you."

Serena thought Nate sounded breathless—and oddly nervous, too—but maybe that was only because he wasn't getting high anymore and she wasn't used to his normal voice. Serena held on to the phone and glanced at Blair and Erik. He was pointing out the window and explaining something to Blair about the layout of the mountain and which runs the sun hit in the morning and in the afternoon. As if Blair cared.

Serena dialed Nate's cell and left a message. "We're totally up for skiing tomorrow," she said. "I'm going to be rusty, though, and we're going to have to stop for hot chocolate and cigarettes every other run, but if you get bored you can always blow us off. Can't wait to meet Georgie. See you at the bottom of River Run at ten-thirty. Bye, Natie." She hung up, popped another chocolate into her mouth, and then crawled across the floor, making a growling sound before opening her jaws and biting the back of Erik's leg.

"Ow!" Erik yowled.

Serena sat back on her haunches. "Can we *do* something?" she asked. "Or are you guys too busy talking in this boring hotel room to, like, go *out*?"

Blair glared down at her friend from her perch on the bed and could barely resist kicking her in the head. Couldn't Serena just butt out and let them talk?

Serena jumped to her feet and grabbed her cosmetics bag out of the splayed-open suitcase lying on her bed. "I'm taking a shower," she announced. "And if you guys are ready to join me for a cocktail afterward, fine. If not, I'll just find some cool, *interesting* people to hang out with, and you can just sit here watching the ski weather report and picking your noses." She knew she sounded kind of bratty, but it was also pretty damned tactful of her to give Erik and Blair time to, like, *do it* on the bed right now while she was showering, if that's what they wanted.

Blair rolled her eyes. Serena was only jealous because all of a sudden Erik wanted to talk to *her* more than he wanted to talk to his little sister. And Blair wasn't about to pass up an opportunity like this. Erik and Serena could see each other anytime.

"I'd better go get dressed," Erik said, hitching up his towel. "You probably have to unpack and everything."

Blair walked over to her bag and unzipped it. She pulled out her bikini and a few pairs of lacy underwear, scattering them on top of the bed in plain view. "I didn't bring much. Actually, I need to rent skis and stuff at the ski shop downstairs."

"Yeah?" Erik paused in the doorway. "I can help you with

that. Tell my sister I'll meet you guys in like half an hour in the lobby. We can get something to eat afterward."

"What about your parents?" Blair asked, remembering that she was a guest on this vacation, and although all she really wanted was to stay in Erik's room and order room service and watch romantic black-and-white movies and rip each other's clothes off, she hadn't forgotten her manners. "Don't we have to eat dinner with them?"

"Nah. They have a ton of friends here. They pretty much always do their own thing. I'm sure they'll want to have, like, one dinner with us, or maybe brunch or something. But basically, we're on our own." His eyes met Blair's in mutual understanding of how good that sounded.

"This is going to be *fun*," she said.

"Yeah, it is," Erik agreed before ducking into his room.

Well, at least it should be entertaining!

was it a gun or just a plain bagel with cream cheese?

"It's like dawn on Sunday morning, and it's only two degrees," Elise complained. "What's with the stakeout?"

"*Shush,*" Jenny whispered. "Here he comes." She grabbed Elise's coat sleeve and dragged her inside the Lexington Avenue dry cleaner's they happened to be standing in front of.

"*Now* what are we doing?" Elise grumbled.

Jenny put her fingers to her lips and crouched down behind a giant yellow bag of laundry. She was wearing dark sunglasses just for the occasion and could barely see a thing in the dingy shop. "*Shhhh.*"

"Can I help you?" the man behind the counter asked. The two girls stayed put as Leo walked quickly past the shop window. His white-blond hair was tucked inside a black watch cap, and he was wearing a bashed-up brown leather jacket with a sheepskin collar that was either very expensive or very old. In his hands were a large coffee in a white paper cup and a white paper bag with something inside it.

Aha! Was it a gun? Jenny wondered. *Someone's hand? A boring toasted plain bagel with cream cheese?*

"Come on!" Jenny leaped to her feet and dragged Elise back out of the shop, trailing Leo down Seventieth Street to Park Avenue.

Leo had never invited Jenny home or even told her where he lived. And when she'd asked him to hang out with her today, he'd said he couldn't, just as he did half the times she asked him. He was so *elusive* that she just couldn't resist spying on him. Leo had a favorite coffee place on the corner of Seventieth and Lex and probably lived somewhere nearby. So that morning, Jenny had dragged Elise out of bed at seven to wait across the street from the coffee shop until he showed up.

"Hey, look," Elise pointed down Park Avenue to a sumptuous-looking doorman building with a green and gold awning. "He's going inside!" She'd acted like the whole spying-on-Leo thing was totally stupid, but now she was getting into it. "Is that where he lives?"

"I don't know," Jenny answered breathlessly. They continued down the block to the corner until they reached a sunny spot. Jenny leaned against the building, waiting for Leo to come out again.

"You're just going to stay here?" Elise pulled a pack of Orbit gum out of her pocket and offered a piece to Jenny.

"What's wrong with that?" Jenny unwrapped the stick of gum and bit off half of it, rewrapping the other half to save for later.

"Well, what if he just sits there and watches TV for three hours? We could die out here," Elise complained.

Jenny chewed her gum and shoved her hands in her black parka pockets. She closed her eyes and let the late March sun drench her face. "It's warmer in the sun. Anyway, what else do we have to do? We're on break. We don't even have any homework."

Elise couldn't argue with that. It totally sucked being one of the only kids in your class who didn't go away skiing or to some beach resort over break. At least Jenny was keeping them busy. She started when she saw Leo's blond head emerge from the building, capless, and without the coffee and white paper bag. *"Hey,"* she whispered, poking Jenny in the arm.

The girls pressed their bodies against the side of the building and ducked their heads, hoping he wouldn't spot them. This time Leo was leading a giant white mastiff on a red leather leash. The dog was wearing one of those three-hundred-dollar Burberry plaid collar-and-coat combinations that only dog-crazy rich people bought, and little pink leather boots.

Oh, my.

Jenny didn't quite know what to make of this. It was completely embarrassing for Leo, but it was also totally intriguing. He'd never even told her he had a dog! She yanked on Elise's sleeve again. "Come *on.*"

They followed at a distance as Leo walked the dog slowly around the block. He was considerate, letting the dog sniff fire hydrants and curbs where other dogs had peed. Then the dog humped its back and did an enormous poop, and Leo dutifully crouched down and picked it up with a little pink plastic baggie he pulled from some sort of baggie dispenser attached to the leash, depositing it in the waste bin on the corner of Sixty-ninth and Madison. After that, he marched the dog around the block to Park Avenue and into the building again.

Jenny leaned against the building in the same sunny spot, totally bewildered by what she'd seen.

Elise stood beside her, chewing noisily. "Hey, I don't know if it's true or not, but you know that site I'm always looking at?" she asked.

"Yeah?"

"Well, it was talking about that fancy party all the rich girls from school went to Thursday night? And it mentioned a boy who was at the party who sounded exactly like Leo. So maybe he's like this zillionaire kid and he's too shy to tell you."

Jenny winced. *Or maybe he's too ashamed of me to bring me home to meet his parents*, she thought miserably. Still, she wasn't totally convinced. Leo didn't act like a rich snob, and he went to kind of an alternative school. If he were a zillionaire, he'd probably go to St. Jude's or some boarding school in New Hampshire or something. "If he's so rich, what's he doing buying his coffee from a deli and walking his own dog?" she countered. Then again, why did his dog wear a collar that cost more than any piece of clothing she owned? God, Leo was even more mysterious than ever!

"Maybe he's a spy impersonating a high-school kid to penetrate some major high-school drug ring," Elise suggested.

"And he has to dress his dog in pink boots as part of his cover?" Jenny said, her eyes trained on the building's entrance. "I don't think so."

Elise did a few jumping jacks to keep her blood circulating. "Well, maybe they're special James Bond dog boots, with, like, torpedoes in them or something."

"Right," Jenny giggled. She kind of liked the idea of Leo being a spy. "And he's a black belt in karate, and he's fluent in, like, twenty-three languages."

Elise bent down and retied her shoelaces. She was getting seriously bored of this. "Who, the dog?

"No, you idiot!" Jenny exclaimed, still watching the door. *"Leo."*

"Who knows?" Elise yawned. She really needed to go back to bed, but she was also secretly hoping that she and Jenny would go back to Jenny's house so she could see Dan again. He was so weird, in a really cute way. "So what do we do now?"

Jenny pulled the other half piece of gum out of her pocket. She spit the old half into the wrapper and shoved the fresh piece into her mouth. Although she hated to admit it, she absolutely loved spying on Leo. "We wait."

Well, at least they're keeping busy.

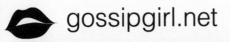

gossipgirl.net

Disclaimer: All the real names of places, people, and events have been altered or abbreviated to protect the innocent. Namely, me.

hey people!

Boys and girls deal differently

Have you ever noticed how when boys are stressed out all they want to do is play video games by themselves for hours or go to the park and kick a ball around with the other boys? When *we* get stressed out we're productive. We clean our closets, shop for the perfect new bag, get our nails done, our eyebrows waxed, and our teeth cleaned. Sitting still is the last thing we want to do, and the thing we most want is to be around people of the opposite sex. Girls—even our closest girlfriends—are too competitive and will only weird us out even more, while boys provide a soothing distraction. But how does it work when all the boys are busy hanging with one another, playing ball? We have two options: Either we can take off half our clothes and create a diversion that's a little more tempting than a round, bouncy ball. Or we can try not to get all competitive and weird on our girlfriends and have a little fun with them. Face it, after you're done kissing that certain special boy, all you really want to do is call your girlfriends, anyway.

Your e-mail

Dear GG,
I'm only thirteen, and when you talk about stuff like college, it still seems really far off to me. Not to my parents, though. It's all they talk about. Like, they're taking me on a college tour over spring break, and they've signed me up for an SAT prep course starting in April. What can I tell them to get them off my back?
—hadenuf

A: Hey hadenuf,

I think everyone can relate. As if we weren't under enough pressure already?! And I know this is going to sound insane, but I recommend a little reverse psychology—it's always worked for me. Become Miss I-Can't-Wait-for-College! Buy all the guidebooks, paper your room with college posters, order college sweatshirts online, buy an SAT prep CD-ROM and use it as your screen saver. Stop watching TV. And if they don't get worried and leave you alone, try dating a guy who's in college. *That* might work. Good luck!

—GG

Q: Dear gossipgurl,

I go to Smale with that boy J's been hanging out with, and it's funny because no one really knows him very well. He takes off after the last bell rings, and no one ever sees him. It's like he's a ghost or something.

—celine

A: Dear celine,

His being a ghost might explain things. After all, ghosts can zip around and pull all sorts of crazy tricks. But would a ghost really bother with school? By the way, I love your name—if that's really your name.

—GG

Sightings

D buying a new black corduroy suit at the **APC** warehouse sale, trying to look French and arty for his new job. **V** trying on khaki pants at the **Gap** with her new boyfriend with the big nose. Since when does she wear khaki? **J** peering down **Park Avenue**, wearing a pair of binoculars and a funny old-man hat. Has she lost her mind? **B** in **Sun Valley** trying on bikinis and buying condoms. Wait, I thought she was supposed to be skiing. And did someone say condoms?! **N** driving a carload of drunk blond men in a black **Mercedes** SUV to a rowdy Mexican restaurant, also in Sun Valley. Doesn't it suck to be the designated driver? And where was his girlfriend—passed out already?

Goody. It sounds like everyone is on their best worst behavior, as usual. Remember to keep me informed. This page is all about you (when it's not about me).

You know you love me.

gossip girl

d is for do as i say, boy

The pockets in Dan's new suit were still sewn shut, and his wet hair was frozen tight and hard against his forehead. "Hello?" he shouted hoarsely into the intercom outside the *Red Letter* offices on Eleventh Street in the West Village. The cigarette he'd been smoking on the walk from the subway had burned down to the quick, singeing his fingers. He tossed it onto the sidewalk, hoping that someone from *Red Letter* wasn't watching disapprovingly from a window. "I'm Daniel Humphrey? The new intern?"

The heavily grated door buzzed, and Dan pushed it open. He wiped his sweaty hands on his pants as he mounted the stairs in front of him. Already he could see the glare of office lights, hear the *tap, tap, tap* of computer keyboards, the hum of fax machines, photocopiers, and printers, and the steady murmur of voices talking on the phone. He reached the top stair and surveyed the open-plan office, full of strange heads bent over desks, talking on the phone and looking busy, busy, busy. Bisecting the white walls was a thin, horizontal red line, making it look like the large room had been wrapped with red ribbon. When he squinted, though, Dan could see that the line was made up of thousands of tiny words painted in red.

He wondered what it said, but in order to get close enough he'd have to lean over someone's desk, and he didn't want to be rude.

He waited for someone to greet him and show him around—someone there must have buzzed him in, after all—but no one seemed to notice him.

Even in his fancy new suit?

He shifted from foot to foot and cleared his throat noisily. Nothing.

"Um," he spoke to the guy sitting nearest him. The guy had dark, slicked-back hair and was wearing a crisp white shirt with French cuffs tucked into neatly pressed black trousers that were probably made by Armani or Gucci or something. There were four unopened minibottles of San Pellegrino mineral water lined up on the desk in front of him. "I'm here to see Siegfried Castle," Dan told him.

The guy looked up and squinted at Dan. *"Pourquoi?"*

Dan frowned. Couldn't the guy just speak English?

"Because I'm his new intern?"

The guy stood up. "And I ham your new boss." He held out his hand, palm up. "Siegfried Castle. Call me Sig—no, actzuelly, I zink you must call me *sir*."

Dan wasn't sure how to handle the palm-up scenario. Boldly he put his hand on top of Siegfried Castle's and turned it around, shaking it up and down like a normal person would.

Siegfried Castle grimaced and removed his hand. "You're a poet, no?"

Dan nodded, his eyes shifting nervously to the other people in the office. They were all looking up now, examining him coldly. He noticed now that everyone else had those little green bottles of San Pellegrino lined up on their desks, too.

And they were all dressed in black and white, just like Mr. Castle. Dan felt like a freak in his light blue shirt and gray suit. "Yes. I had a poem in the Valentine's Day issue of *The New Yorker* last month. Maybe you saw it? It's called 'Sluts.'"

Siegfried Castle didn't seem to hear him, and Dan wondered if there was some sort of rivalry between *Red Letter* and *The New Yorker*. Maybe he'd committed a horrible faux pas by mentioning the competition. "Now. I show you my out box. My in box. My files. Show you the slush pile. Show you the photocopier. The phone. The fax. You sit there. I call you for things. We eat at one-thirty in conference room. You will order our food." He was pointing around the office, and Dan realized that Mr. Castle wasn't going to show him anything else or introduce him to anyone. The tour was over.

The phone rang, and Siegfried Castle sat down again and pointed at it with a neatly manicured finger. Dan picked up the phone. "Hello?" He winced, realizing he should have said something more professional. "May I help you?"

"Who the fuck are you?" the voice on the other end said in an English accent. "Get me the Zigster, pronto."

He held the phone out to Mr. Castle, who he noticed had a few gray hairs and was probably older than he looked. "It's for you, I think."

Dan sat down in what was presumably his chair in the corner, facing the wall. There was nothing on the desk. No computer, no phone. Not even any San Pellegrino. He wondered if he should go around and introduce himself to the other people in the office, but he didn't really want to bother them while they were working. He squinted up at the red line of words running along the wall, but the more he looked at them, the more they seemed to dance and blur together. He glanced sideways at Mr. Castle's out box. It had a letter in it.

"Would you like me to mail that for you?" he asked.

Siegfried popped a cigarette into his mouth and flicked open his silver Zippo lighter. Then he threw the unlit cigarette into the trash can beneath his desk. "Go ahead," he said spitefully, as if he couldn't wait to get rid of Dan. "Also, I need caviar." He pulled a hundred-dollar bill out of his pocket. "Gourmet Garage on Seventh Avenue. *Not* beluga. It's zee black one in the blue tin."

As if *anyone* would know what he was talking about?

Dan took the money and the letter and went outside. The envelope wasn't stamped, and he had no idea where the post office was, but surely there was one nearby, and he could smoke a cigarette while he was looking for it.

Ten blocks later he still hadn't found the post office, but he'd smoked four cigarettes on a pier overlooking the Hudson River. "I have to get back," he told himself, and tossed his cigarette into the water. But how could he go back with the envelope in hand, looking like a dope because he couldn't figure out where to buy a stamp?

He leaned against the railing, and before he could stop and think about what he was doing, he tossed the envelope into the swirling brown water. It floated on top for a minute, turned beige and wet-looking, and then sank.

Whoops!

Dan turned quickly around and strode across the pier and up Eleventh Street. Maybe when he got home tonight, he'd look online and locate the nearest post office to the *Red Letter* headquarters. How important could that one letter have been, anyway?

He shoved his hands in his pockets, felt the crinkle of the hundred-dollar bill, and remembered the caviar.

"Fuck."

Inside Gourmet Garage, there were stacks of tinned black caviar and about eight different kinds with blue labels. Dan grabbed the most expensive one and headed over to the register.

"Dan?"

He turned around. It was Elise, Jenny's friend. She was carrying a baguette that was about three feet long, and she had flour on her face. She looked sort of cute, actually, except that Dan suddenly noticed she was much taller than he was, by like a foot.

"What are you doing here? Jenny said you were starting your new job today."

Dan pointed to the little tin of caviar motoring along on the black rubber conveyor belt toward the cashier. How could anything that small cost seventy-four dollars? "My boss sent me out to buy some stuff."

Elise watched as he paid for the caviar with the hundred-dollar bill and then tucked it and the change into his APC storm coat pocket. "Wow," she breathed, impressed. "Well, anyway, I just went over to your new office to bring you some cookies. I was bored, and I thought maybe you'd like a treat on your first day." She smiled shyly as she paid for her baguette. "I always write better when I have something good to munch on."

Dan wasn't quite sure what to make of this. "I have to get back," he told her, and pushed open the door to the street.

"Okay." She walked with him to the corner with the baguette tucked under her arm. There was flour all over her black wool pea coat. "I need a cab. I was just buying my mom some bread. Our family practically lives on Coke and French bread. My dad calls it the Wells Diet."

Dan smiled. The diet worked. Elise was pretty skinny. He squinted up at her in the cold noon sun. Elise had brought him cookies. She had cute freckles and was gangly and tall and had a baguette under her arm. Standing there in her black pea coat and black ballet flats, she looked extremely French and poetic. He could definitely write a poem about her.

She waved the baguette at a passing cab. "Hey!" The cab stopped, and she turned to say good-bye. "Jenny and I might watch movies or something later. Maybe I'll see you at your house?"

Dan took a step toward her. "You have flour on your cheek." He daubed at it with his thumb and then kissed the spot. "There."

The corners of Elise's lips turned up in a tentative smile. "Thanks." The cabbie honked his horn. She tucked the baguette more snugly under her arm. "I left the cookies on your desk. They're good, I think. Okay, see you," she added before hopping into the backseat of the taxi.

Petite mignonette, Dan began to write in his head as he walked back toward the office. *Sweet coquette.* He wasn't even sure if those were real French words, but they sounded like a flirty little French girl who carried bread under her arm and brought you cookies. The kind you wrote songs and poems about and kissed on the cheek. Elise was only fourteen, after all. She was no Mystery Craze, but she obviously adored him, and at least she was *around.*

He lit another cigarette and walked back to the office at a leisurely pace. So far this work thing wasn't so bad.

As long as he stayed out of the office.

v helps her parents find art

"Look, dad, an old sled," Vanessa called. She'd made the mistake of mentioning how much old stuff people in New York leave out on the sidewalk—she'd actually found a pair of perfectly good old-fashioned roller skates that way—and now she was patrolling the streets of Williamsburg, helping them hunt for found-art treasures.

Arlo shuffled over to the red plastic sled and picked it up. It was cracked down the middle and covered with puffy stickers of turtles. The bottom of it was stained and discolored from the days of dog pee it had endured.

"It might smell," Vanessa warned.

Arlo shrugged and dropped it into Ruby's black metal shopping cart. Already they'd found a blue plastic fishbowl, a white chef's hat, and an ashtray made out of thumbtacks.

"What we really need is something big," Gabriela said as they continued on. "Something profound."

Vanessa trailed them grudgingly, wondering what her mother meant. Another horse? A supersized cheese grater? She kicked a crushed empty juice box away with her foot and sat down on a stoop while her mom and dad conversed with the owner of an ancient pickup truck parked outside what looked like a fisherman's shack in the midst of a block of warehouses. Then her mom walked over and sat down next to her.

"Arlo's found a kindred spirit," she remarked, smiling at her husband from afar. "I think he's going to be a while."

Today Arlo was wearing his wool poncho over Bermuda shorts and tennis shoes with no socks. His knees were bluish white and knobby, and his shins were bruised from knocking around in his forge up in Vermont, making mobiles out of old wheelbarrow carcasses or deer antlers. Vanessa marveled that her dad had ever found someone who could look at him the way her mom did. Talk about kindred spirits!

"So what happened to that wonderful shaggy little boyfriend of yours?" Gabriela asked. She pulled the rubber band out of the end of her long gray braid and combed her paint-stained fingers through her hair.

Vanessa grimaced. Part of the reason she kept her head shaved was that her mother's hair grossed her out. "You mean Dan?"

Gabriela reached up and began to massage the back of Vanessa's neck. Vanessa winced—she hated to be touched without an invitation—but her mother didn't notice her discomfort. "I always thought you two would wind up getting married or something. You reminded me of Arlo and me."

Vanessa hugged her knees, enduring the massage. "Dan's joined the police force," she said, knowing how much her parents resented law enforcement.

"No kidding." Gabriela let go of Vanessa's neck. She divided her gray hair into three thick clumps and began to braid it again. "He was such a marvelous talent. Such a rare, keen eye for beauty. And so loyal."

Loyal? Maybe not.

"Ha!" Vanessa fumed. Dan would be nowhere if she

hadn't recognized how good his poem was and submitted it to *The New Yorker*. "Actually, Dan's not becoming a cop," she admitted. "He just stopped being nice. Like, it's okay to walk all over people as long as he can get a good poem out of it." She glanced at her mother to see if the comment had registered. "He's an asshole," she added.

"True artists are forever accused of being assholes," Gabriela sighed. "You mustn't be so hard on us." She fastened the end of her ponytail with the elastic band from the bunch of broccoli Ruby had cooked last night. "You know who the real assholes are?"

"Who?" Vanessa asked, standing up. Her father was walking toward them now with a stinky old fishing net in his hands, grinning eagerly, like he couldn't wait for show-and-tell.

"The Rosenfelds," her mother replied. "That comment Pilar made the other night about how she doesn't even recycle? What kind of person doesn't recycle?!"

Um, lots of us.

"Jordy's nice," Vanessa ventured quietly.

"But those glasses he was wearing? They probably cost as much as our car! If you ask me, he should have spent the money on a nose job."

See, even peace-loving hippie freaks can't resist a little nasty gossip.

Vanessa snorted. Considering the fact that her parents drove a Subaru wagon that was older than she was, Jordy's glasses probably cost *way* more than their car. And if her mom really detested the Rosenfelds so much, Vanessa couldn't wait for her mom to find out whom she'd invited to Ruby's gig later that night.

A certain expensive-glasses-wearing, long-nosed boy, perhaps?

stroke of brilliance found on intern's desk!

When Dan finally made it back to the office, he was buzzed in again only to find the place completely deserted. He deposited the change for the caviar on Siegfried Castle's desk and continued past the row of desks and down a short hallway. At the end of the hallway was a closed door. Dan could hear voices on the other side of the door. He knocked softly.

"Come in," Siegfried Castle commanded.

Dan pushed open the door. The *Red Letter* staff was seated around a conference table, eating cookies and sipping San Pellegrino water out of those little green bottles they all seemed to like so much. A printed copy of Mystery Craze's brand-new memoir translated into German was lying in the middle of the table. The cover was white with a picture of a flamingo on it. Not the whole bird, just the legs, with one leg folded up at the knee.

"We zought if you didn't come back with zee caviar, we could still enjoy your cookies," Siegfried Castle explained. He nodded at the petite, middle-aged woman seated next to him. "This is Betsy. Zat's Charles. Zat's Thomas. Zat's Rebecca. Bill, another Bill, und Randolph," he said, continuing around the room and introducing everyone at a ridiculously rapid pace.

Randolph was also Dan's middle name, and he despised it. He nodded and smiled politely. Everyone was dressed exactly like Mr. Castle, in pressed white shirts with French cuffs. It was like they were in some sort of cult.

"Sorry I took so long. There was a really big line at the post office," he lied. Normally he wasn't into lying or throwing out people's mail, but something about having a job made him want to rebel. "Anyway, here it is." He set the tin of caviar down on the table in front of Mr. Castle.

The famous editor peeled the label off the tin and stuck it on the table. Then he tossed the caviar into the wastepaper bin near the door.

Hello?

Dan wasn't sure whether to sit down or not. Obviously they were having some sort of meeting, and obviously he'd bought the wrong kind of caviar so—

"So tell us vhat you tink of Mystewy Cwaze," Mr. Castle interrupted his thoughts. "Everyvun here tinks she's some sort of prophet, even zee vimmen!" The guys around the table laughed lasciviously.

"She's a freaking sex goddess," Randolph called out, chomping on his cookies.

Dan was still standing, suffocating in his coat. He sat down in the empty seat next to Mr. Castle and stared at the empty plate where Elise's cookies had been. "Mystery and I are pretty good friends," he said quietly. "She's very . . . *accomplished*."

The guys in the room laughed loudly again. All of a sudden Dan had a feeling he wasn't the only one there who'd slept with Mystery.

"She's a pretty good poet, too," Rebecca remarked. She had pointy ears, like an elf's. "I can't believe she's never been to school."

"An orphan zat's never been to school, raised by wolves, vill do anything and zen write about it later. No vonder she's already famous," Siegfried Castle remarked dreamily. He jotted something down on the purple pad lying in front of him on the table.

Dan fiddled with the threads sewn across his suit pants pocket. He wasn't really sure what this meeting was about. What he really needed was a cigarette and a cup of coffee, and to write down the poem about Elise before he forgot what he wanted to say.

He gestured toward the German version of Mystery's memoir. "I haven't read her book yet, but I'm sure it's good."

Siegfried Castle picked up a pile of papers from off the floor and tossed them on the table in front of Dan. "Zat's all cwap—vee warely take anyting from submissions. But I vant to read it, anyway."

Dan looked at the pile. He'd always thought everything in *Red Letter* came from submissions. "How do you do it, then?"

Everyone laughed. "Silly boy. Vee just ask our friends to write tings, or maybe vee find someting vee like written on zee bathroom wall," Mr. Castle declared, as if it were the most obvious thing in the world.

Dan picked up the pile of papers. "Do you want me to set aside the ones I think are good?" he asked, confused.

"Just read zem and zen trow dem away!" Siegfried Castle yelled, his face red and angry-looking. "Out! Out!" he cried, pointing at the door. He swiped the empty cookie plate from off the table and shoved it at Dan. "Out!"

Dan hurried out of the room, carrying the plate and the poems back to his empty desk. His entire body was shaking, and he was worried he might cry. Instead, he began flipping through the pile of poems, reading quickly. Some of them were pretty awful, but some of them were original and brilliant. He thought of asking Mr. Castle what he thought was wrong with the poems. Or maybe he could leave the poems he liked in Mr. Castle's in box with a note asking him to reconsider them. But then again, the less he had to do with Siegfried Castle, the better.

When he'd gotten control of himself again, he pulled a blank piece of paper out of the stack near the printer and clicked open his pen, jotting down the first few lines of the poem that had been in his head all afternoon.

> *Petite mignonette, sweet coquette*
> *I taste your cookies, your bread*
> *You fill my plate*

The last line sounded familiar, like maybe he'd already used it in another poem. He crossed his legs, pondering, and heard the sound of a toilet flushing. He could pee, he decided. Pee and then finish the poem. He got up to go to the bathroom. Inside, there was something written in Latin on the wall in red ink, but he couldn't decipher it.

When he got back to his desk the piece of paper with his poem on it was gone, but the entire staff was still in the conference room.

Dan didn't dare investigate. He could only hope his fragment of a poem would be published under "Anonymous" in the next issue of *Red Letter*. Eventually, he could leak the information that the poem was his, and the literary world would clamor for more. He'd publish a book—or maybe ten books—and become world-famous, just like Mystery Craze.

Although maybe not quite as notorious.

I, mystery man

Jenny and Leo held hands throughout the entire movie and kept holding hands as they walked out of the theater. Jenny hadn't even paid attention to the movie. All she could think the entire time was, *He's going to take me home afterward. We're only five blocks away from that big doorman building on Park. And then I'll meet his dog and his mom and her personal trainer and their ten maids . . .*

"So, I was thinking maybe we could walk over to the Guggenheim now." Leo smiled down at her with his cute cracked-tooth smile.

If he was so loaded then how come his parents didn't get his tooth fixed? Jenny wondered. Then again, she was glad they hadn't. "It's after eight. Aren't all the museums closed by now?"

"They have these once-a-month things at night," Leo explained. "And it's kind of cooler, you know, seeing the paintings when it's dark out."

If Jenny had been thinking properly, she would have thought this was just about the best thing anyone had ever said. First of all, how cool was it that she and Leo were both into art and museums? Second of all, how cool was it that he knew about these funky nighttime art happenings and that he wanted to take *her* to one?

But all Jenny could think was, *He's not taking me home! What's wrong with me? What's wrong with* him? *What's his story?*

"Do you have any pets?" she demanded suspiciously as they crossed Second Avenue and headed east toward Fifth.

"Pets? No. Why?" Leo wrapped an arm around her shoulders. "Brrr. You warm enough? Do you want my scarf?"

Another heart-meltingly romantic gesture, but did she notice?

No pets? Jenny brooded, too distracted to be bothered by the cold. *But why would he lie? And how come he's trying to change the subject so quickly?*

"Well, here we are."

The ghostlike coil-pot structure that was the Guggenheim Museum hovered above them in the dark. "Kiss, Kiss," a banner proclaimed, flapping over the museum's entrance. Leo blushed when he noticed Jenny looking at it.

"Come on, let's go in."

Jenny opened her purse to pay for her half of the admission, but Leo motioned for her to put her wallet away. "That's okay. I'm a member. We can get in free."

A member? Well, well, well. And hadn't Elise said that Leo had been seen at that big Frick Museum benefit on Thursday night? His family probably *owned* the Guggenheim.

They wound their way up the graded halls of the museum, stopping at the first painting on exhibit. It was Marc Chagall's *Birthday,* a painting of a woman holding a bouquet of flowers, kissing a man who is flying in the air above her head. The woman looked as if she had just been doing something boring, like setting the table, when the man swooped down and caught her lips with his.

"I love the blue," Leo said, studying it. "You would think blue would make it cold, but it doesn't. It warms it up."

"Mmm." Jenny wasn't listening to a word he said. She was studying his profile, his hair, his clothes, his shoes, his fingernails, looking for a clue, some sort of explanation.

Leo glanced at her, blushing again. He took her hand. "May I kiss you? I mean, before we look at the next one?"

If she hadn't been paying attention before, she was now.

"Oh! Um. Sure." Jenny took a step backward and almost lost her balance.

Leo held her hand even tighter. "I've got you."

Jenny let him pull her toward him, and she lifted up her face to meet his. What they did next was no mystery at all, although she kind of wondered where he'd learned to kiss so well.

If only she could stop thinking so much.

that prelaw geek is looking pretty hot

"You know he must really like you if he came all the way out here on a night like this," Ruby whispered in Vanessa's ear just before her regular Monday night gig with her band, SugarDaddy, was about to begin.

"He's just here for the music," Vanessa replied sarcastically.

Jordy Rosenfeld was standing in the doorway of the dark, crowded club, unzipping his green Columbia ski parka. His weirdly long nose was red and dripping from the cold, and his bright yellow turtleneck and khaki pants stood out like strobe lights amongst the black-clad native Williamsburgers.

Normally the sight of a guy like him might have made her cringe, but at this point Vanessa didn't care how yellow his turtleneck was. And his nose was actually kind of sexy and distinguished, if you looked at it from a certain angle. She stood up and waved him over.

"Hello, Mrs. Abrams," Jordy greeted Gabriela. "How are you, Mr. Abrams?"

Vanessa's parents were wearing matching Greenpeace T-shirts, tight black leggings, and Birkenstocks with white tube socks. They could have been a piece in one of their art shows.

Still-life of hippie freaks.

Gabriela shot her daughter a look of confused surprise. "Hello, Jordy. Vanessa didn't tell us *you* were coming tonight."

"That's because I wanted to keep it a secret." Vanessa flashed Jordy her version of a come-hither smile, which was actually just a normal-looking smile, since Vanessa didn't smile much.

Jordy unzipped his jacket and sat down next to her. "I got my paper done."

"Then you deserve a drink," Vanessa told him. She motioned to the bartender, tapping on her nose and pulling her ears in a series of pretend signals. SugarDaddy played so regularly at the Five and Dime, it was practically their second home. Vanessa had even had a fling with the old bartender, who now guided whitewater rafting trips in New Zealand.

The bartender came over to see what Vanessa's new friend wanted.

"Do you have Baileys Irish Cream?" Jordy asked.

Arlo was watching the band as they went through their sound check. SugarDaddy was made up of four Irish guys with pale faces and far-away looking eyes, and Ruby, who yelled and shook her ass a lot, even though she wasn't the lead singer.

"Eating goober peas," Ruby said quietly into her mike, testing the sound. Arlo grinned, looking extremely proud.

Gabriela got up to go the bathroom. "I hope they start soon. Arlo and I promised these nice people we met on the subway we'd do a chanting session with them at midnight."

The bartender brought over the glass of milky beige stuff on ice, and Jordy took a sip. "I like it," he said simply.

Gabriela came back from the bathroom, her long gray hair rebraided and pinned Heidi-style on top of her head. She'd put on ChapStick—her version of makeup—and taken off her tube socks.

The lights dimmed, and Ruby began to growl into the microphone and slap her bass. Then the band broke into one of their signature tunes, "Canada Is the Future."

Jordy glanced around the crowded bar, his huge narrow nostrils flaring. Vanessa noticed the tag was sticking out of the neck of his yellow turtleneck. *Made in China,* it said.

Gabriela pointed at it. "Did you know that most of the textiles made in China are produced by prisoners from Thailand who are tortured and starved?"

Jordy stared at her.

"Your shirt was made by victims of mass trade," Gabriela lectured.

Vanessa was sure there was some validity to what her mother was saying, but Jordy's shirt was already ugly enough—they didn't have to talk about where it was made.

SugarDaddy broke into one of their famously long drum riffs. Ruby yelled along with the drummer's noise, something about assholes in minivans.

"You don't know how disappointed I was to hear your mother say she doesn't recycle," Gabriela droned on. "I was thinking you and your parents should maybe come up to Vermont for a little retreat. It's very pure up there. It might help remind them what's sacred."

Jordy smiled politely. "I'll mention it to them. But really, the only reason my parents don't recycle is because their apartment building has an incinerator, and it's just easier to chuck everything down the chute. I basically live on shrimp-flavored ramen noodles and coffee, so I don't have anything to recycle, anyway."

Gabriela stared at him in frightened alarm.

Vanessa grinned. Yes, Jordy was the Antichrist, and he was getting cuter and cuter by the second. She inched her chair a little closer to his as SugarDaddy struck up one of their weird, bouncy dance tunes.

Vanessa leaned over and whispered in Jordy's ear, "Any second now I'm going to kiss you."

The corners of his lips turned up, and he took another sip of Baileys.

Gabriela nudged Arlo's leg with her bare toe. "Come on and dance, darling. I need to blown off some steam."

But Arlo was so transfixed by the musicians, drool was collecting in the corners of his mouth. Vanessa thought he looked like a baby watching the circus for the first time.

She inched even closer to Jordy and held up her face, angling it a little to avoid running into his nose. "I'm going to kiss you *now*," she whispered before her mother could drag Arlo out of his seat.

Then she pressed her lips against his, tasting the Baileys and the difference between kissing him and kissing Dan. And it was kind of . . . yummy.

sex is better après-ski

"Are you sure you're not cold?" Serena asked Blair for the fourth time. Blair was wearing only her pink Eres bikini top underneath a white cashmere cable-knit cardigan, and black Miss Sixty stretch cords.

Not exactly high-performance mountain gear—but that depends on your definition of performance.

Blair leaned against Erik's shoulder as she made another attempt to jam her ski-boot heel down into her bindings. "Darn, it won't go in." She grinned sheepishly as Erik knelt at her feet to help. He was wearing a fuzzy Patagonia fleece jacket over an adorable hand-knit Aran sweater and tight black ski racing pants that showed off the definition of his long, sexy thighs. No, she wasn't remotely cold, but thanks for asking.

Serena batted at the snow with her ski pole, eager to get out on the slopes and away from whatever was going on between her big brother and her best friend. It was kind of cute watching Erik pretend he didn't know Blair was flirting with him. But then again, it kind of wasn't.

Serena zipped her sensible-but-sexy lavender one-piece Ellesse ski suit up to her chin and pulled her gray cashmere flap hat down over her ears. If Nate didn't get there soon, she was going to hit the chairlift alone. There was a whole mountain full of cute boys just waiting to fall in love with the way she cut her turns. She just had to get out there.

"Good." Erik stood up and pulled on his heavy-duty black leather ski gloves. "How does that feel?"

Blair leaned on her poles and bounced her knees up and down like a go-go dancer. "Okay," she ventured timidly. "But what if I fall?"

Erik shoved his mirrored Scott sunglasses up on his nose. He looked as if he'd been skiing there all season, even though he'd only just arrived. "I won't let you fall," he promised, with a grin that implied he'd be holding her hand all the way down the mountain.

Serena rolled her eyes and pulled her Smith goggles down, ready to ditch them both and leave a note for Nate with the chairlift attendant, but then she saw Nate's golden head bob up the snowy path from the road, his pot-leaf snowboard and Georgie's skis propped effortlessly on his strong, boatbuilder's shoulders. Georgie was at his side, her waist-length almost-black hair fanning out behind her like a cape. She was wearing a mink-lined dark denim jumpsuit that looked like it had been made especially for her by Tom Ford. Even her hat and her brown leather ski boots were trimmed with mink.

"She's prettier than I remember," Serena said quietly, but Blair was too busy pretending her stomach hadn't done a funny little dip at the sight of Nate and his new girlfriend even to hear her.

When they were still a few hundred yards away, Nate heaved the skis off his shoulder, and he and Georgie stepped into them effortlessly. Then they skied over, gliding gracefully across the snow like figure skaters.

"Hey. Good to see you." Nate had been up half the night watching Georgie do naked Jägermeister shots in the hot tub with the Dutch snowboarding team, so he wasn't lying. Morning couldn't have come soon enough.

"Wow!" Georgie enthused when she saw Blair. "You're brave."

Blair gave Georgie the once-over and unzipped her cardigan a few inches. "Thanks," she replied, even though she wasn't exactly sure what Georgie meant.

"I've got the same one in white," Georgie said, pointing to Blair's bikini top.

Both Erik and Nate stared at Blair's small but nice chest, imagining how much better Georgie's bigger and nicer chest would look like in a white version of the same top.

Erik held a ski pole out to Blair. "Come on, I'll tow you."

Aw, how *cute*!

They were just about to join the long line to the chairlift when Chuck Bass coasted by on his new Burton snowboard. "Hey," he greeted them. "I've been getting pointers on the half-pipe from the Dutch team. Those guys are the bomb!"

All five of them watched Chuck glide on into the ski school queue, which got to cut the rest of the line. "Come on!" he called over. "I've got a ski instructor pass!"

None of them even wanted to know how Chuck had finagled a ski instructor pass. They didn't even mind skiing with him if it meant they got to cut the lines.

Exactly the result he'd been going for.

All the major lifts in the resort were high-speed quads, taking four people up the mountain at a time. Serena and Georgie were the first two in line, and although it pained Blair to ride next to Georgie, she couldn't exactly yell, "Stop!" when Erik joined them.

Swoosh! The chairlift swooped under their bums and lifted them off their skis and into the air.

"Whee!" Serena and Georgie cried in unison.

"Whoa." Blair clutched Erik's arm. Even after all these years of skiing, chairlifts still made her nervous.

Nate and Chuck were right behind them, their snowboards banging together as they sank into the chair.

"Got any weed?" Chuck unzipped the chest pocket of his shiny dark purple Bogner ski suit with its weird fox fur zip-on collar and pulled out a silver flask. He offered it to Nate. "Brandy?"

"I don't get high anymore," Nate insisted stubbornly. He squinted at Chuck's boots. They were exactly the same as his, but Chuck's snowboard was hot pink, with the words *Chiquita Banana* written across the top of it. It was definitely a girl's snowboard, and Nate sort of suspected Chuck was wearing a woman's ski suit. That wasn't even gay, it was just plain weird.

Ahead of them, smoke curled up into the air above Georgie's mink hat. Nate could only hope that the others would be sensible enough not to let her do anything too illegal on the chairlift.

Chuck pulled a Marlboro out from behind his ear and lit it. His jawline was shadowy with black stubble, and it looked like he might be growing some experimental facial hair. "I heard Blair and your new girlfriend had a major catfight over you up at rehab in Greenwich."

Nate waved Chuck's cigarette smoke away. He was kind of grooving on the pointy tops of the pretty dark green pine trees growing out of the soft white blanket of snow below them. The smoke was ruining it.

"I also heard Georgie and Serena went to boarding school

up in New Hampshire together and got kicked out at the same time. They were caught doing it. Like this." Chuck grabbed his crotch and ground his pelvis into the chair, his tongue lolling disgustingly.

"I doubt that," Nate said, although he wasn't so sure. He'd never actually heard the whole story of why Serena had gotten kicked out of Hanover Academy at the beginning of the school year, and he barely knew anything about Georgie. The two girls hadn't given any hint of recognizing each other when they'd met just now, but then again, girls often played it cool until they had a chance to talk and figure things out.

Up ahead of them, Georgie and Serena were lighting their second clove cigarettes. "I only smoke these on the lift," Georgie explained with the air of someone who smokes something different at every altitude. "They taste better up here."

"Mmm," Serena inhaled. She turned around to check on Nate and Chuck. Nate was staring straight ahead, while Chuck smoked and gabbed. "What a cute couple," she joked.

Georgie giggled. "See, even Chuck thinks Nate is cute."

Blair didn't say anything, but she secretly hoped Georgie's fur hat would catch fire and she'd fall to the ground in a heap of burning fur.

Serena gave Nate the finger. Then she grinned and blew him a kiss. Georgie turned around and did the same thing but in the opposite order.

"You know you love us!" the two girls shouted.

Blair slid her arm through Erik's as the chair headed toward the steep downhill ramp where they had to unload. Getting off the lift was even worse than getting on.

"Keep your tips up, and hold on to me," Erik coached her gently.

She did as she was told, keeping a steady grip on his arm as they glided down the ramp side by side. Then Erik made a neat little turn and skidded to a stop. Blair slammed into him and sat down hard on the backs of her skis.

Oof!

Erik grabbed her and quickly pulled her to a standing position again, holding her in his strong, comforting arms. "Don't worry, nobody saw."

Blair giggled. God, his eyes were blue. And he was so . . . *capable.* Then it dawned on her. *I'm going to lose it to Erik on this trip!* Why not? They'd known each other all their lives. It made perfect sense.

Just like it makes perfect sense to wear a bikini top in the snow?

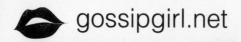 gossipgirl.net

hey people!

About that rumor that's going around . . .

Like there's only one. But you know the one I'm talking about. Apparently some people are saying a certain blond senior who got kicked out of Hanover Academy in October wasn't alone in the scandal. She had a partner: an infamous dark-haired girl from Connecticut. Well, I've done some research, and it does seem that said Connecticut girl *was* enrolled at Hanover for a brief time, although the date and circumstances of her departure are unclear. She's been to six schools in four years, and since she's so busy at rehab, it doesn't look like she's going to finish high school any time soon. And it's not like they're best friends or anything, since they've never been seen together around town For now, let's just say this deserves further investigation. And believe me, I'll investigate.

Your e-mail

Hey Gossip Girl,
My family spends every spring break in Hawaii because I have four little brothers who love to surf—I know, my life is hell. Well, it *was* hell. Now it's not so bad. Last night while I was babysitting my brothers by the pool, this boy with short little dreadlocks who was babysitting another kid in the pool started talking to me. I know it's fast, but now I think I'm in love. We believe in all the same things, like total vegetarianism and making music instead of war. The only thing is, I live in California and I'm going to UC Berkeley next year, and he lives in New York and is going to Harvard. Do you think it's wrong to lose your virginity on spring break with a boy you barely know?
—atfirstsight

A:

Dear atfirstsight,

Yours is a question that keeps coming up so I guess I'd better answer it before it's too late! First of all, you said so yourself: You and Mr. Total Vegetarianism live on opposites sides of the continent. It may seem convenient now, but why not wait to see if either one of you cares enough to travel that far for your big night. Then you'll really know it's true love, if not true lust! Second of all, Spring Break has only just begun. Mr. T.V. might have looked good last night by the pool, but Mr. Even Better could be scooping up tofu bacon at the breakfast buffet table tomorrow morning. And because you don't want to be known as the Vegetarian Ho of Waikiki, it might be nice to keep your options open and stick to above-the-navel activities. I have nothing against kissing more than one boy over Spring Break, or even over the course of a day! Have fun!!

—GG

Sightings

J snooping around the **Upper East Side** with a pair of binoculars around her neck. It's pretty safe to say she wasn't bird-watching. Her tall blond boyfriend, **L**, in **Bendel's** again, buying ladies' leather gloves in size large—way, way too big for **J**. **D** walking uptown from the Village, chain-smoking and browsing in bookstores. Our friends in Sun Valley watching the Dutch snowboarding team do tricks on the half-pipe while they drank hot mulled wine on the sidelines. **S** and **G** were chatting away, **B** was sitting in **E**'s lap, and **N** and **C** were sitting very close together, holding hands and discussing which Dutch snowboarder they thought was cuter. Just kidding. But really, skiing is all about what happens between runs.

Don't forget to tell me every naughty thing you're doing.

And guess what? I'm already tan!

You know you love me,

gossip girl

d avoids the obvious with *e*

"I can't believe you've got your hands in there," Jenny cried, scrunching up her nose as Leo mashed raw eggs, butter, sugar, flour, and cocoa powder together with his bare hands. It had been his idea to make brownies, but of course they had to make them at her house, not his. Jenny didn't know when she'd ever get to see his house.

"My mom taught me this. It's the only way to get it really well mixed without using a beater." Leo's red-and-white-checked shirt sleeves were rolled up to the elbows, and he was biting his lower lip in concentration—the utter picture of adorable—as his hands worked the contents of the large ceramic bowl.

"Oh," Jenny replied, sifting in another cup of flour. "Does your mom like to cook?" Anyone who lived in that fancy apartment building on Park Avenue must have a full-time chef.

"Kind of. Mostly she just likes making brownies."

Aha. See? Cooking was just another hobby, like dressing her dog in designer clothes and getting her face Botoxed.

Leo removed his finger from the sweet batter and held it out to Jenny. "Taste?"

Jenny was so preoccupied with the thought of his mother

baking brownies on the cook's night off that she opened her mouth and gave his finger a good long suck.

Oh!

"Oops. I guess I'm interrupting something," Elise observed from the kitchen doorway. "You guys are so cute," she added hollowly.

The downstairs buzzer had rung only a few minutes ago, but after buzzing Elise in, Jenny had become so preoccupied with Leo's brownie-making skills, she'd completely forgotten about her friend. She picked up the wooden spoon she'd gotten out to mix the brownie dough with in the first place. "Want to taste it?"

Elise wrinkled up her nose. "Nah. I'll wait till they're cooked. Is Dan home?"

Jenny shrugged. She hadn't noticed him leave.

"I'm pretty sure he is, because I think I smell smoke." Elise headed down the hall to Dan's bedroom. "Call me when the brownies are done!"

Dan was lying on his bed, trying to think of a synonym for *desire* that rhymed with *clock*. *Sock, mock, jock, rock.* He hadn't gotten very far.

"Can I come in?" Elise asked from outside his bedroom door.

"Sure." Dan sat up and closed the little black notebook he was writing in. Elise was wearing a black turtleneck sweater that made her look serious and older somehow. "What's up?"

"Nothing." She sat down on the end of the bed. "What are you writing?"

Dan hopped off the bed and chucked his notebook on his desk. He reached for his pack of Camels and lit one, inhaling deeply as he shook out the match. "Quick, a word that rhymes with *clock*."

"Tock," Elise shot back.

Dan stared at her. "But that's not a real word. It doesn't mean anything without the 'tick-tock' part."

"No, I guess you're right." She stood up and went over to his desk, towering four inches over Dan. Her height definitely made her seem older. So did the careful way she dressed, with her T-shirt tucked neatly into her belted jeans and her cardigan all buttoned up. Instead of being prissy, it conveyed a sort of confidence, as if, "I am a woman and this is how it's done."

She flipped open one of his notebooks. "So this is where you write everything?"

Dan's first impulse was to snatch the book away from her, but Elise wasn't Vanessa. She wasn't going to make fun of one of his lesser poems or push him to send one of his better ones off to a famous magazine. "Yeah. I don't like working on the computer because I wind up deleting stuff I might use."

Elise nodded and rifled through the pages.

"Hey, I got you something." Dan opened the black messenger bag he always carried and pulled out the book of writing exercises he'd bought for Elise earlier that day. "To thank you for the cookies."

Elise took the book and examined it. "Wow, this is like homework. As if I don't have enough already."

"But it's really not," Dan said, taking the book back and turning to one of the exercises. "'Avoid the obvious. Make a list of all the clichés you've ever heard of and never use them in your writing.'" He looked up. "See? It's fun!"

Elise looked at him like he was insane. "I guess it's probably more fun than watching your best friend suck brownie batter off her boyfriend's fingers." She picked up a pen and turned to a free page in one of Dan's black notebooks. "What exactly *is* a cliché, anyway?"

Dan liked how unembarrassed she was about her ignorance. "You know, like 'love at first sight' or 'hard as a rock' or 'blind as a bat.' All those things you've heard a thousand times."

"Uh-huh." She sat down on the bed and wrote something. Then she passed the notebook to Dan. "Okay, your turn."

He was going to write, *What goes around comes around*, until he saw what Elise had written: *Why did you kiss me on the street today?*

He stubbed out his cigarette in an ashtray and gripped the pen hard to steady his fingers. *Because of the cookies*, he wrote. *And because of the bread.* Actually, he didn't know exactly why he'd kissed her. It had been a spur-of-the-moment thing. He handed the notebook back, and Elise read what he'd written without looking up. Then she wrote something underneath it and passed the notebook back.

Kiss me again?

Dan walked over to the door and pushed it closed. He tossed the notebook on the bed and turned to Elise, kissing her hard on the mouth as he yanked her T-shirt out of her jeans.

Elise let out a little cry and took a step backward. Dan let go of her. All of a sudden Elise didn't seem so old anymore. Her blue eyes were wide, and her smile was less a smile than a terrified grimace.

"I'm sorry."

"It's okay," she said, more to herself than to him. "I'm okay." Dan noticed a roll of pale baby fat hanging over the waistband of her jeans. She saw him looking at it and quickly tucked her T-shirt back in.

Loser, Dan scolded himself. Elise was only fourteen, and he was nearly eighteen. He was worse than slimy. He was a total asshole.

Elise was still standing there waiting for him to kiss her again, and all of a sudden he felt sort of pissed at her, too, for even thinking this might be a good idea.

He turned his back and sat down in front of the computer, jiggling the mouse. "I think the brownies are probably done," he told her hoarsely.

Elise stayed put, so Dan started checking his e-mail. He kept his back turned until finally he heard her walking toward the door.

"I thought you wanted to be my boyfriend," she mumbled, her throat choked with tears. A moment later, Dan heard the front door of the apartment slam shut.

He picked up his notebook and turned to a fresh page. *Because of the cookies and because of the bread*, he wrote, and then stopped.

It was a little difficult to feel inspired.

v doth protest too much

"I know you're working on a paper right now and we just saw each other last night, but do you want to go get dinner?" Vanessa practically shouted into the phone.

"What, like right now?" Jordy asked.

"Yes. *Now.*" Tantric chanting emanated from the living room, where Vanessa's parents were hosting a gathering of artist friends for an evening of "sparking the creative flint." Whatever the hell *that* meant. "I can meet you somewhere in your neighborhood," she offered. "Anywhere is fine."

"Wow," Vanessa said when she arrived. Despite its name, Bubba's—an Italian place near Columbia—was actually nice. She'd expected tables covered with red-and-white-checked plastic tablecloths and sides of fries served with every dish. Instead, the tablecloths were white, and there were candles and old jazz playing. It was only five-thirty, and the restaurant was empty. But even that was romantic, in a very traditional way.

Jordy was already seated at a table and had ordered a bottle of red wine. The waiter took Vanessa's black wool jacket and helped her into her chair. "I feel so mature."

Jordy shrugged like he was used to this. After all, he was in college. "I like your lipstick."

Vanessa couldn't tell if he was joking or not. Jordy wore a constant pleasantly arrogant expression, making it extremely difficult to gauge his emotions. If only his nose acted as some sort of barometer, getting longer or shorter depending on his mood.

Not that she really wanted his nose to get any longer.

"My parents are having some sort of freak-fest chanting session with a bunch of other so-called artists in our apartment." Vanessa told him, scowling as she opened her napkin and put it on her lap. "I can't wait for them to leave."

Jordy took a sip of wine, pressing his thin lips together as if he really enjoyed the taste of it. His expensive glasses were on the table, and Vanessa saw for the first time that his eyes were light golden brown, like a lion's.

Way to notice a boy's eye color *after* you've already kissed him!

"I think your parents are amazing," he said. "I mean, it takes a lot of effort and courage to be that . . . *out there*."

Vanessa's thick brown eyebrows shot up. "I'll say." She scraped her chair forward and put her elbows on the table. "You know, when I was little I was a scab-picker. Any little nick or insect bite I'd pick away at until it bled and bled. And you know what my mom said? She said I ought to save the scabs so my dad could make a piece of artwork out of them. Isn't that just the most insanely twisted thing you've ever heard? I mean, most moms would be worried about scarring, or they'd take their kid to a shrink. My parents, all they care about is themselves and their 'work.'"

Jordy shrugged. "Maybe she was joking."

Vanessa frowned and opened her menu. Antipasti, primi, secondi, dolci. *Joking?* She'd never heard her mother be remotely jocular. "I don't think so."

Jordy watched her as she scrutinized the menu. "Still, I really admire them. I mean, the way they're letting you and your sister live on your own. Not many parents would do that."

"No. Not many would," Vanessa agreed with a scowl.

"I'd kind of like to go up to Vermont and see how they live," Jordy added eagerly.

Vanessa looked up from her menu in alarm. "Why?"

"I don't know. I haven't met that many people who are . . . you know . . . *different*. I'm just curious, I guess." He took a sip of wine and did that thing with his lips again. "So, my mom kind of mentioned that you had a pretty serious boyfriend. Is that, like, all over, or what?"

Vanessa flipped her menu closed without deciding on anything. She wasn't really hungry, anyway—she'd just wanted to get out of the house. "Yeah, it's over. We're not even friends anymore." Normally her voice had a bitter fuck-you bite to it, but just now it had quavered with emotion. "Not that I mind," she added tartly.

The waiter came and Vanessa ordered a salad. She felt like one of those skinny blond girls in her class at Constance who only ate dry lettuce and Jell-o.

Jordy ripped a piece of bread off the hunk in the basket on the table. "So did you break up with him, or the other way around?" With long, delicate fingers he dunked the bread in the little bowl of olive oil.

She'd never really thought about who'd broken up with whom. In fact, there'd never been an official breakup. After she'd caught Dan fooling around with that Mystery Craze person on stage in a poetry club, she'd refused to return his phone calls. If anyone had broken up with anyone, she'd broken up with him. But did that mean that maybe he hadn't meant to break up with her at all?

It was almost too confusing to think about.

"I-I guess I sort of inadvertently broke up with him," she stammered. "I mean, he *was* cheating on me." It felt weird talking to another guy about her relationship with Dan. It felt weird talking to someone else period, since the only person she'd ever really talked to was Dan himself. But Jordy's arrogant sincerity was just that: sincere. And it was kind of hard to cop an attitude in the face of all that sincerity. Vanessa felt her lower lip begin to tremble as tears welled up in her big brown eyes. Oh God. She hated it when she cried, especially in public. What was wrong with her?

There, there. It's happened to the best of us.

Jordy put his glasses back on. "I'm sorry. We don't have to talk about this if you don't want to." His wan cheeks flushed. "I was kind of only asking for selfish reasons, anyway." He took off his glasses again and set them carefully on the table next to the olive oil. Then he lifted his gaze, his golden eyes gazing straight into hers. "I really like you, Vanessa."

Miles Davis was playing and the candles flickered. All of a sudden Vanessa felt like she was starring in one of those badly made romantic films that most girls cried over and she couldn't stand. "I like you, too," she sobbed, mortified. If she were with Dan, she would have suddenly burst out laughing and told him to go fuck himself for making her cry. But Jordy wasn't Dan. If she told him to go fuck himself, he'd probably do it.

Well, not literally. But we know what she means.

She wiped her damp face on her white linen napkin, smearing Ruby's lipstick all over it. "Sorry. I guess my parents are really stressing me out." She put down her napkin and took a gulp of water. "So tell me something about Columbia. Like, what's your favorite course?"

As if she genuinely cared. It was pretty obvious now that Jordy was only interested in her because her parents were *alternative*, and she was only interested in him because he was so completely *un*alternative. Besides, her mind was too occupied with its most recent download to pay attention to a word of Jordy's reply. And the information her mind was so busy processing was that she was still in love with Dan.

she just wants somebody to love

After a full day of skiing, followed by an hour of watching the Dutch Olympic snowboarding team tear up the half-pipe, the group retired to the lodge at the base of the mountain for some well-deserved happy-hour pitchers of beer. The lodge had a roaring fire, a piano player, and cocktail waitresses wearing denim vests with nothing underneath.

Serena sat down next to Jan, one of the seven snowboarders. The whole team was blond and athletic and handsome, but she'd chosen Jan because when he boarded he stuck his thumbs out in a very peculiar cute way, like he was giving the entire mountain the thumbs-up.

"Are all the girls in New York as beautiful as you and your friends?" he asked with his charming Dutch accent.

Serena giggled. She was a sucker for charm. "You guys are so lucky—getting to do this every day."

Jan laughed and took a swig of dark amber beer. "We are not always snowboarding. I go to university in Minsk. I'm studying to be a dentist."

"Oh." Serena had imagined that the whole team lived together in a cabin on top of a mountain in the Alps somewhere, snowboarding all day and getting drunk together every night. She'd thought it would be cozy, being the only girl in the group. She could cut their hair for them and make French toast for breakfast. At night they'd curl up by the fire and tell ghost stories. "What about the others?" she asked, wondering if she'd just chosen the wrong guy.

"Conrad is married to an Italian girl—they live in Bologna. Franz is my roommate at university. Josef, Sven, Ulrich, and Gan all live in Amsterdam."

Amsterdam was supposed to be a really cool city. Serena looked across the table at the four boys. They were all equally hot, blond, and athletic.

"In the gay student housing," Jan added.

"Oh," Serena replied, forcing herself to smile.

Better luck next time.

"Would y'all like anything else?"

"I'll just have another Coke, please," Nate told the cute, Ugg-wearing cocktail waitress after Chuck had ordered another three pitchers of Sun Valley ale for the table. Georgie had already drunk an entire pitcher on her own. He would probably have to carry her home.

"I can't believe I made it all the way down a double black diamond without falling," Blair gushed for the forty-fifth time. She sipped her beer delicately and grinned at Erik. "You're a much better teacher than any of those ski instructor guys."

The truth was, she'd slid sideways down almost the entire run, screaming the whole way, but at least she'd managed to keep her bare cleavage free of snow. That was the important part.

"You just kept getting better and better," Erik replied. She had buttoned her cashmere cardigan over her bikini top but her jeans were low slung, and with the way she was sitting up straight and sort of leaning into the table, he could see the top of her ass. It was nice.

"I'll bet you a hundred bucks I can chug my beer faster than you can chug yours," Georgie dared Serena.

Now that there was no one to flirt with, Serena was happy to have something to do. She pulled her long, ski-wild blond hair back behind her and tied it in a knot. Then she picked up her glass. The rest of the table watched in gleeful anticipation.

Well, *most* of the rest of the table.

Nate crunched an ice cube between his teeth. He could just imagine where this was going. Both girls were going to get completely wasted, throwing up all over everybody, and then they'd be out of commission with hangovers for the next couple of days. His sexy lips drooped forlornly over the rim of his Coke glass. No more skiing. No more fun.

"Show her how it's done, Georgie!" Chuck goaded them on.

"Oh yeah?" Serena lifted her glass to her lips. Then she noticed Nate shaking his head, and she moved it away again. "What am I doing? You're, like, bred for this. Your whole family is full of famous alcoholics."

"Thanks a lot!" Georgie cried. She nudged Serena with a bony elbow. "Go on, drink!"

Serena set the glass down. "It's not worth it. If I chugged this I'd puke all over the table. And you'd totally beat me, anyway."

Georgie shrugged, then threw her head back and downed the whole pint of beer in one go. "Fuck you, I won," she burped when she was done.

"Good for you," Nate breathed. Everyone turned to look at him.

"Natie's just mad because we haven't had a chance to do it yet," Georgie crowed. "I'm always too fucked up!"

There was an awkward silence. It was hard to know how to respond to that.

Blair looked at her watch. "Maybe we should get back to the lodge so we can have a sauna before dinner." She wasn't sure if the sauna in the lodge was coed or not, but the idea of being in a hot, steamy room with Erik, dressed only in towels, was very appealing. He could rub her back with lavender-scented oil and—

"Yeah, my quads are in pretty rough shape," Nate agreed, rubbing his thighs. He glanced miserably at Georgie. "I could really use a soak in the tub."

Georgie clapped her hands together, her eyes shining giddily. "Let's *all* go back to my place and get in the tub!" She was so hyper all the time, Nate wondered if the rehab clinic had her on some kind of antidepressant or something he didn't know about. All he knew was that the beer didn't seem to slow her down.

Chuck was already zipping up his coat in preparation to leave. "I'll make everyone my famous peach schnapps cocktail!" He lifted up his shirt and batted his eyelashes. "Chucky's Fuzzy Navel."

Sounds delicious.

Nate still hadn't figured out why Chuck seemed to be living at Georgie's house when he had a perfectly good hotel suite at the Christiana, the luxury hotel in town where his parents were staying.

The piano player began to play an old Billy Joel song, and the lights dimmed. Happy hour was over. Serena could kind of tell by the look on Nate's face—and Georgie's comment— that he and his girlfriend needed some time alone. She pushed her chair back and pulled her sweater on over her head. "It sounds tempting, but we actually have to get back. I told Mom we'd meet her and Dad for dinner at the lodge at seven-thirty. We need to take showers and stuff."

Georgie's face fell. "Oh, come on. Can't you just call your parents and tell them you're busy?"

Easy for her to say. She basically didn't have any parents.

Serena glanced at Erik, and they did that wordless communication thing that only close siblings can do. "Sorry," she said firmly.

Nate didn't know how he'd wound up with a senseless girl like Georgie when his former girlfriend and best friend-who-happened-to-be-a-girl seemed like the most sensible girls alive.

Georgie got up and then sat down in Nate's lap, letting her head fall back against his shoulder. Her dark silky hair smelled like beer and cloves. "We'll just have to party without you, then."

Blair smirked. "Too bad." Her smirk morphed into a winning smile. "Should we go then?" she asked Erik. "I'm starving!"

Chuck sat down primly on Georgie's knees, wriggling his bottom back and forth. Then six of the Dutch snowboarders got up and piled into Chuck's lap, squashing Nate completely. All except Jan, who was watching Serena get ready to go with a droopy, abandoned-puppy look on his handsome face.

"Enjoy your dinner," Chuck called out. "We'll just have a manwich!"

Blair and Erik hastily collected their gloves and sunglasses and headed for the door. Serena tucked her hat under her arm, following close behind. Then she heard Georgie let out a shriek, and she turned around. The entire group had fallen off the chair and collapsed in a giggling heap on the floor. Jan had jumped on top of them, and even Nate seemed to be smiling despite himself.

Serena looked on longingly. She had always been right there at center of all the fun, but now she was stuck with Blair and Erik, who were so entranced by each other, they barely acknowledged her existence. Still, her parents would be waiting. She couldn't exactly blow them off and sabotage the rest of her vacation. She turned for the exit again. There were five more days of vacation left, and she was resolved to have a good time no matter what. Wasn't that what she'd always been known for?

Well, yes, among other things.

just when you think you know someone . . .

Leo dried the last bowl and set it on the dish rack to dry. "I have to go."

Jenny put down the brownie she'd been munching on. They'd baked twenty, and there were only twelve left. She licked the crumbs off her fingers and gazed up at Leo with her long-lashed brown eyes. She was tired of guessing. She wanted to know the truth. "Where?"

Leo leaned against the cracked yellow linoleum kitchen counter and fiddled with the buttons on the dishwasher. Marx, the Humphreys' fat black cat, was splayed out on the grubby kitchen floor, asleep. Leo cleared his throat, and Marx flapped his tail up and down in annoyance.

"I have errands to do," he told her vaguely.

"Well, can I come?"

He kicked his feet around and blew out of the side of his mouth. "It's really not very interesting."

Jenny wasn't convinced. "You're not, like, hiding something from me, are you?"

He laughed. "Like what? I'm really Spider-Man?"

Jenny's face turned red. She walked over to the fridge, opened the door, then let it slam shut again. "I don't know.

I just think it's weird, the way you're always busy doing stuff and you never talk about it."

Leo put his hands in his pockets. His light blond hair looked transparent under the glare of the harsh kitchen light. "If you really want to come, you can come."

Jenny tried to keep her face calm. This was it. She was going to find out all the secrets that lay behind Leo, mystery boy and megazillionaire. "Okay."

They took the Ninety-sixth Street bus across town and then walked down Park toward the building on Seventieth Street. The avenue felt deserted in the dark, with everyone away on vacation.

"It's just a couple more blocks," Leo told her. Jenny's whole body tingled with anticipation.

When they reached the building with the green awning, the door man tipped his hat to Leo. Then they rode the elevator straight up to the penthouse.

"Whoa," Jenny gasped, when the elevator doors opened up onto the parlor. The room was done in black and white and gold. A round gilt table stood in the middle of the black-and-white marble floor, with a giant white vase in the shape of a swan on it, filled with black roses. To the left was a sort of gold-painted railing and stairs down to a room so big, it could only be a ballroom.

"I know. It's kind of insane," Leo agreed. "Here, Daphne!" he called

Immediately Jenny heard the scratch of nails on the floor. The giant white mastiff she'd seen Leo walking before trotted into the parlor, wagging her tail elegantly. She went over and licked Leo's hand. "Good girl."

Jenny watched in dumb amazement as Leo opened the coat closet door and retrieved Daphne's Burberry coat and matching collar. The dog waited carefully while he buckled them on. Then he knelt and Velcroed those horrible pink leather booties over her paws. "There. We're all set to go."

Jenny still couldn't figure out why Leo's parents didn't just get one of their maids to walk the dog, but she wasn't about to say anything, especially not when Leo obviously loved Daphne so much.

"We'll just take her for a little spin around the neighborhood. I have to pick up some hairspray for Madame at the drugstore. Maybe you could hold her while I go in?"

"Okay." Jenny kept her eyes on Daphne's boots. He called his mom *Madame*?

They stopped in front of Zitomer on Madison. Jenny took the plaid canvas leash while Leo went in to get the hairspray. She bent down, and Daphne offered her a pink-booted paw. "I bet he lets you sleep in his bed," she said. "I bet you're allowed on all the furniture."

Leo came out of the store carrying a huge shopping bag full of lots of bottles of the same kind of Redken hairspray. He chuckled. "Madame uses this stuff a lot." He took Daphne's leash, and they walked briskly back to the building with the green awning. "I still have to feed her and water the plants and stuff. It's really not very exciting. Do you want to get a cab home, or can we walk you to your bus stop?"

Jenny didn't know what to say. It was almost as though he didn't want her in his house. "I guess I'll just take a cab," she answered stiffly.

"Okay. Walter will help," Leo said, nodding at the doorman. He kissed Jenny's cheek. "Don't eat any more brownies today or you'll get sick. I'll call you later, okay?"

Jenny smiled grimly at him and walked over to the curb to catch a cab. It was a while before Walter could snag one, and as soon as he closed the door behind her and she gave the driver her address, Jenny collapsed in the backseat, sobbing.

The cab got stuck waiting for the light at the corner next to Leo's building, and she glared at it miserably through her tears. Just as the light changed and the driver turned the corner, Leo walked out of the building and headed uptown.

"Wait," Jenny ordered the driver. "I changed my mind. I'm getting out." She paid him quickly and leaped out, hurrying up Park Avenue after Leo.

He kept walking uptown until he reached Eighty-first Street. Then he turned right, crossing Park and then Lexington. She jumped behind a pile of garbage bags as Leo turned in at a three-story brownstone and walked down two steps to the below-ground entrance. He got out his keys and unlocked a black metal gate. When he pushed it open Jenny could see two metal garbage cans with a racing bicycle leaning against them. Then he closed the gate and disappeared inside.

She remained crouched behind the garbage for half an hour, half expecting him to come out again with another dog in tow. But he stayed inside, and she thought she could see a TV flickering behind the thick gray curtains in the windows. Finally, she gave up and went home.

Just when you think you know someone, you find you don't know them at all.

d sends more mail downriver

On his second day of work, Dan didn't even try to find the post office. Instead, he stood on the end of the pier and one by one dropped the six letters from Sig Castle's out box into the Hudson River. One of the letters was addressed to Mystery Craze, care of Rusty Klein, which gave Dan a smug sense of satisfaction. For all he knew, Mystery was so friggin' internationally famous, she might even get the letter, washed up on a beach in Sardinia, where she would be giving a reading to a bunch of drunken fishermen.

He stared into the brown, swirling water, thinking about all the girls he'd ever had anything to do with. Serena and Vanessa and Mystery and Elise. Not all of them had gone so well, especially that last little episode with Elise. But next year he'd be off to Brown or U. Mass or whatever college would take him, and he'd have four very different experiences with four bizarrely different girls to carry with him always. Wasn't that what being a writer was all about—having experiences and translating them into meaning with words? Something like that, anyway. He was a published writer. He knew what he wanted to do with his life. That was a hell of a lot more than most people his age could say. So what kept him feeling so . . .

unhinged? It was like he was constantly looking for something, just looking and looking.

Sig Castle had asked him to buy some kind of special rice paper in a store down in Chinatown once he was finished with the mail, so after finishing his fifth Camel, Dan walked over to West Fourth Street and took the subway downtown.

It was raining lightly and the street vendors on Canal were hawking fake Burberry umbrellas and those disposable plastic rain ponchos only desperate tourists wore in sudden downpours. Dan meandered down the wide, crowded street, taking his time. The air smelled of wet newspaper and fish from the Chinatown fish markets. It made him think of Vanessa. She was quintessentially perverse, a lover of bad smells and ugliness. It was what he most loved about her.

Liked, Dan reminded himself. How could you claim to love something about a person you weren't even talking to anymore?

He stopped and watched a vendor demonstrate a battery-operated pink plastic toy shaped like a UFO with three little Japanese girls sitting on top of it, spinning and revolving to a Japanese pop song that sounded sort of like SugarDaddy—Vanessa's sister's band—on speed. The toy was just the sort of device Vanessa would use to open one of her films. She'd zoom in on the toy and then cut to a girl dancing by herself in a club. Vanessa created meaning with images the same way Dan did with words.

He walked down Broadway to Pearl River Mart, a huge store that carried just about everything, from plastic Buddhas to rubber boots. He found the nearest thing to Siegfried Castle's favorite ultrathin, ultrasoft, impossible-to-get-a-paper-cut-from rice paper and then headed back over to Canal to the vendor with the pink UFO.

"I'd like to buy that, please."

"I have a new one here," the guy said, ducking down to pull a mint green UFO toy out from under the table the pink one was spinning on.

"No. That one," Dan insisted, pointing at the pink toy. Pink was such an un-Vanessa color, she'd have to see the humor in it, and at least he knew it worked.

"Two dollars," the man said, even though the cardboard sign taped to the side of the table said, "$3!!" "It's on sale."

Dan handed over some of Sig Castle's change from the rice paper. His boss was such an asshole, he got a certain satisfaction from fucking him over every chance he got.

"Have a good day." The guy handed him a bright blue plastic bag with the pink toy in it. Dan was pretty sure there was a post office over on Bowery Street only a few blocks away. He could mail the package to Vanessa from there before taking the subway back up to work.

Funny, he'd never thought to mail the *Red Letter* mail from there!

Sig Castle had made it sound crucial that he get his rice paper before lunch, but it was even more crucial that Vanessa get her UFO, Dan decided. It was imperative.

"Send it next-day," he told the postal worker behind the counter after he'd bought a box and taped it up. "It's important."

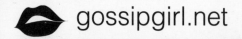

hey people!

Those people we meet on vacation

Face it, you wouldn't be caught dead with them at home. Their shoes are bad, their jeans are sad, their hair needs help, and they say "wow" a lot, but you eat breakfast with them every day and invite them out with you at night. Don't feel guilty if the above scenario sounds weirdly familiar. Even I've been guilty of palling around with someone for the duration of my vacation and then ditching them the minute I return home. It's got something to do with the herd instinct, although I'm not sure what. Maybe I'll learn about it next year in Psych 101.

What about those two?

My sources say this is definitely not the first encounter between the infamous Greenwich heiress and our favorite perfume model. The two were fast friends at Hanover their junior year but had a fight over a boy in France the summer before they were both kicked out. I'm pretty sure there's more, but instead of making up a lot of hooey, I'd rather wait for the skeletons to come tumbling out of the closet, and I'm sure they will.

Sightings, lots of 'em

V walking from Manhattan to Williamsburg, picking up trash with her parents and looking miserable. **D** taking out a recycling bag filled with hundreds of little bottles of unopened **San Pellegrino** water outside a building on Eleventh Street. **B** taking off her skis in the middle of a run in **Sun Valley**, just to see if a certain boy would hike all the way back up the run to help her put them back on. **S** and **G** in the bathroom at the bottom of the mountain in Sun Valley, with the entire **Dutch Olympic snowboarding team**. Playing kissing games? **C** and **N** on the lift up to Sun Valley's half-pipe. Also playing kissing games? **S** and the Dutch Olympic snowboarding team posing for a **ChapStick** ad at the top of the mountain.

She's not the only one keeping busy on her vacation! Enjoy it while it lasts.

You know you love me.

gossip girl

upper east siders party
sun valley style

"Okay, I'm ready," Serena said after smearing a little moisturizer on her face and running a brush through her still-damp hair once or twice.

Of course she looked beautiful—she couldn't help it—but she could have given the locals a real treat and at least worn a little lip gloss.

"Well, I'm not." Blair leaned over the bathroom sink to apply some mascara. A white towel was wrapped around her head and her freshly polished nails were barely dry. "Aren't you even going to blow-dry your hair?"

"Nope." Serena looked at her watch. Erik was waiting for them in the lobby, and she'd barely gotten a chance to talk to him alone since they'd arrived. "I'll meet you downstairs, okay?"

"Fine," Blair answered distractedly. She didn't know why Serena had to be in such a hurry. This was their first Sun Valley party, and she for one wanted to look good. Erik had been so attentive and was always so completely adorable that tonight might just be the night she said, Yes, oh yes! "What's the rush, anyway?"

Serena blew out her breath. "What's the point of making an effort? It's not like I'm going to be flirting with somebody's brother all night!"

Blair screwed the top back on her mascara and glared at her friend's reflection in the bathroom mirror. "So you're mad at me because of Erik?" She dug around in her cosmetics bag for her bronzing powder.

Serena kicked the door frame with her fuzzy sheepskin boot. "I'm not mad. I'm just . . ."

Jealous?

She sighed noisily and turned around to yank her powder blue parka from the hook by the door. "I'll see you downstairs," she mumbled, as she hurled herself out the door.

"Don't worry," Blair called after her. "I'm moving back home when we get back!"

"Aren't you cold?" Nate took off his well-worn, navy blue Brown sweatshirt and offered it to Georgie. He slept in the sweatshirt for luck sometimes. As if the Brown admissions office was going to overlook the fact that he'd been busted by the cops for buying weed just because he liked to sleep in their sweatshirt.

Georgie was walking around in her orange sorbet La Perla panty-and-bra set while Chuck Bass, Josef, Sven, Ulrich, and Gan played mah-jongg on Xbox. *Maybe they* are *all gay*, Nate thought hopefully. Even so, he didn't like it when Georgie walked around in her underwear. She was too . . . too . . . *naked*, and her nakedness was supposed to be reserved for herself and *him*. After all, she was his girlfriend. Well . . . wasn't she?

"Why don't we go upstairs?" he whispered suggestively in her ear. He'd imagined that he and Georgie would spend the majority of their time in Sun Valley in bed having lots of sex. But he'd never even taken his pants off in her presence. Not once. And it wasn't that Georgie was actually a serious prude under all that flaunting and nakedness. She was just too busy being crazy and guzzling mood enhancers to lie still for a second and let him kiss her.

"What's upstairs?" Georgie asked, lighting a cigarette. Her long silky brown hair was pulled over one pale shoulder and her long pale legs were crossed, *twice.*

Only seriously skinny girls can do that.

Nate shrugged. "I just thought we could . . . you know . . . hang out."

Any normal girl would have looked into his emerald green eyes and gone all prickly and faint at such an invitation. But Georgie was too screwed up even to notice how cute and irresistible he was.

In other words, she was an idiot.

She cocked a suspicious eyebrow at Nate. "You didn't smuggle in weed without telling me, did you?" she asked hopefully.

"Nah." He reached out and touched her hair, smoothing it over her bony shoulder. "I just thought we could use the privacy," he said, his cheeks turning adorably pink at the suggestion in his voice.

Georgie swung her legs over the arm of the wooden chair she was sitting on. It had been carved by Shoshone Indians out of birch trees and then painted orange.

Butt-ugly, but probably worth a fortune.

There was a honk outside. Georgie swung her feet to the floor and swiped Nate's sweatshirt out of his hand. "Guess I should put something on," she mumbled, yanking the thing over her head as she headed for the front door. Her white butt cheeks peeked out from under the navy blue sweatshirt, somehow making her look even more naked than before.

"Thank God you're here," she told the bemused delivery guy. She pulled a bottle of Stoli out of the crate on his dolly and cracked it open. Then she grabbed the remote control for the ten-disc CD player and clicked it on. An old Blondie song came on—"The Tide Is High." "You can set up the coolers out by the hot tub." Georgie pointed at Nate with the bottle of Stoli. "He'll show you where it is."

Down in the lobby of the Sun Valley Lodge, Erik was talking to a bunch of ski patrol guys about the day's big rescue. Some dude had been showing his girlfriend how to ski backward and had skied right into a tree. A branch had impaled him right in the ass.

"It was pretty gnarly," Serena heard one of the ski patrol guys say.

"What was?" she asked, climbing into Erik's lap. He draped his long arms around her, and she burrowed her cheek into his chest, hungry for attention. "Mmm. You smell nice and clean."

The ski patrol dudes sipped their beers and looked on enviously. If only they each had their own model-gorgeous blond sister to snuggle with.

"Hey, where's your friend? The one with the cute little . . . haircut?" one of them asked.

Serena sat up and perched on Erik's knee, her baby-blue-Ugg-bedecked feet just grazing the carpet. She tugged on the legs of her Habitual jeans. Usually people were too busy looking at *her* to ask about Blair. But Blair did put a hell of a lot more effort into her appearance than Serena did, so maybe Blair deserved the attention.

"She's upstairs, getting ready." She elbowed Erik in the belly. "You want to go up and check on her?"

Erik kind of liked that the ski patrol guys had noticed Blair, since he and Blair were so clearly going to be getting it on very soon. He elbowed Serena back.

"Ow!"

The two siblings exchanged fierce glances. "I didn't say anything bad," Serena insisted sulkily. Erik's fierce look turned into an amused grin. "What?"

"I think someone's here to see you," he whispered.

Serena looked up to find Jan, future dentist and blond Dutch Olympic snowboarder, gazing at her soulfully. "I was hoping to escort you to the party."

The ski patrol guys stepped back to make room for him. Serena slid off her brother's knee. This wasn't exactly the kind of attention she'd been hoping for. "Um, we're waiting for Blair."

Erik gave her a little push from behind. "Why don't you two run along?" He gestured to the ski patrol guys. "I invited these guys to the party. Blair and I can get a lift with them."

Just then the elevator doors *bing*ed and slid open.

Ladies and gentlemen . . . Queen of the Mountain!

Blair had fastened a little gold heart barrette in her hair and was wearing the jade chandelier earrings Les Best had given Serena after she'd modeled in his runway show. She was also wearing Serena's light blue cashmere pullover, which was fine because Serena had been planning on giving it to her, anyway. It was a little tight in the chest, which was also fine. Blair liked it like that.

So did the Sun Valley Ski Patrol. They nudged one another and shifted their feet and mumbled noisily, like animals in a barnyard.

"Hey. You look fantastic," Erik said, liking the way the other guys were ogling her. He held out his hand possessively. "Ready to go?"

Blair was glad she had taken her time getting ready. She was even wearing the plain white cotton Hanro underwear that Serena always made fun of, calling them her "grannypants." But the truth was, Blair was always more comfortable in her granny undies than in all the fussy, lacy panties and thongs she owned. And she looked better in them, too. They were what she imagined herself wearing when she was being undressed.

And someone was definitely going to be undressing her tonight.

still life with toothbrushes

Jenny was so confused by what had happened with Leo earlier that evening that she stayed up late, painting a still life and sorting out her thoughts. As usual, there were no fruit or vegetables in the fridge except for a thousand-year-old moldy orange, so she painted toothbrushes and a bar of Dove soap instead.

It seemed entirely possible that Leo did not own a dog and did not live in that stunning apartment on Park Avenue.

Maybe he's just a normal, everyday person, she thought to herself as she carefully touched up the blue bristles on Dan's toothbrush. *Just like me.* Actually, she still didn't know what he was. Why didn't he just make it clear instead of playing games?

She glared down at her canvas. "This is dumb," she grumbled, and tossed it into the trash can under her desk. Everything was dumb. All of a sudden she just felt so . . . *dumb.*

And dumb people need company.

"Oh, so now you have time to talk to me?" Elise said when she picked up the phone.

"I'm sorry," Jenny allowed. "I've been acting stupid."

"That's okay." Elise's voice softened. "Anyway, I don't see why you're making such a big deal out of this. I mean, if he was so rich and his mom was this crazy person who dressed up her dog, he probably wouldn't be such a good boyfriend to have. Right?"

Jenny thought about this. "How would you know?" she asked suspiciously. "How many boyfriends have you had?"

Elise didn't answer right away. Jenny had touched on a sore subject. "Actually, I thought your brother was going to be my first boyfriend, but I guess not."

Jenny snorted. "Like that would ever work. You don't smoke, and you don't even like coffee."

She could feel Elise smiling on the other end, and it felt good that she'd made her friend smile. "Anyway, I think you should stop thinking of Leo as something he's not and just see if you like who he actually is."

Jenny crouched down and pulled the smudged, wet still life out of her wastepaper basket. Maybe if she didn't think of the toothbrush painting as a still life but as a painting with toothbrushes in it, it would work better. She might even add something not so still to it, like Marx the cat. She lay down on her stomach and pulled up the corner of her pink bedspread, looking for him.

"So . . ." Elise said. "Are you going to call him or what?"

Marx wasn't there. Jenny stood up and went over to her computer. "No. He likes e-mail better." She sat down, an idea forming in her head.

She was going to invite herself over to Leo's house—at least, she was pretty sure that basement apartment on East Eighty-first Street was his house. This e-mail was her warning signal. She was going to find out once and for all who he was and what he was all about—whether he liked it or not.

The phone still pressed to her ear, she went online and started to type.

"So you really don't think Dan and I could have worked?" Elise persisted. "He was writing a poem about me, I think."

Jenny could have told her all about how Dan was still in love with Vanessa and how all the poems he wrote were really about Vanessa and him, even when he pretended they were about someone else. Also, she'd bet anything Elise would get bored with his "I'm a tortured, miserable soul" bullshit after about ten minutes.

"No way," she answered distractedly. "Sorry, let me just finish this."

"That's okay. I think I'm going to e-mail your brother right now and tell him what a jerk he is."

"Good idea," Jenny agreed.

Now both girls were typing away at their keyboards as they breathed ferociously into their phones.

When you have a tough message to get across, it's always good to have backup.

e-mailing boys is so much easier than talking to them face to face

Dear Leo,
I know this seems like a strange thing to say, but I really feel like you've been hiding something from me and I don't know. I really like you a lot, and I think you like me. So how come you've never invited me to your house? The thing is, I know where you live now. So I'm coming over tomorrow at six, which is when you're usually finished walking Daphne, I think. Okay. See you then.

                                    Jenny

Dear Daniel,
First of all, I think you are a real jerk for leading me on, because you know I'm younger than you and less experienced, and you should watch out whose heart you break, because it could come back and bite you in the ass. Also, it's so obvious you are still hung up on the first and only girl who would

be stupid enough to be your girlfriend. Your
sister didn't even have to tell me that—you
are just so transparent, it's like you're
writing on tracing paper. There, I can be
poetic, too. Write that, asshole!
Your nonfriend and best critic,

Elise

b tries to keep her eyes on the prize

The door to Georgie's house stood open. No Doubt was blasting out of both the indoor and outdoor speakers, and there were clothes strewn all over the front steps. Four boys with long hair were walking around in their underwear eating wild-mushroom potstickers and showing off their snowboarding muscles. When Blair and Serena walked in with Erik and Jan and the ski patrol guys, they turned around to gape and smile.

"Where's Georgie?" Serena asked, desperate to find the heart of the party before Jan-the-dentist tried to get her alone.

"In the hot tub," the boys answered in unison.

Blair stayed in the living room while Serena went out the patio doors in search of their host, with Jan trailing after her. Erik went over to the bar and began to mix drinks. He'd taken a bartending course last semester—the most useful thing he'd learned in college so far.

Blair noticed that Nate was sitting by himself on a leather sofa in the corner of the living room, sort of picking at his toes. He was wearing his broken-in navy blue Brown sweatshirt and a pair of tattered yellow St. Jude's gym shorts. With his wavy golden brown curls and sparkling green eyes, he looked like a sad little boy. Blair wanted to sit down next to him and ask him why he was picking his toes and looking so sad at his girl-friend's party, but then Erik came over and handed her a glass filled with something swirly and orangey-pink.

"Mai tai. Careful, it doesn't taste it, but it's almost *all* liquor."

"Thanks." Blair took the glass. Normally she preferred vodka tonics, but she'd drink anything Erik made for her.

"I'm going out to sit in the tub," Erik said. "Wanna come?"

Blair shook her head. "No thanks." The idea of jumping into the hot tub with Georgie and whoever else was in there really wasn't all that appealing. And she didn't want Erik to think she couldn't fend for herself at a party. Besides, there was a whole table of catered food standing only ten feet away. If Erik went outside, she'd have a chance to stuff her face without worrying about whether he thought she was a big fat pig or not.

A girl needs fuel, especially when she has a long night ahead of her.

As soon as Erik left, she grabbed a plate of spring rolls and plopped down on a love seat next to a guy with shoulder-length brown hair, who was smoking a joint.

He looked up at her and smiled. "You board?"

Blair had no clue what he was talking about. "No." She took a deep breath through her nostrils. She never got high, but she was feeling sort of nervous all of a sudden, and all the stoners she knew were so mellow. Maybe a few hits off this guy's joint were just what she needed. "Is that pot?"

The guy smiled again and looked at the roach in his hand. "It *was*. Sorry, it's kaput." He wasn't wearing a shirt or shoes, and he still had his ski pants on. They were bright green, with reinforced knees.

"So how do you know Georgie?" Blair asked, still chomping her food.

"Who?"

Blair could feel Nate watching her from across the room. Maybe he thought she was sharing this guy's joint.

Oh, the irony.

"Where do you go to school?" she asked, figuring the guy must be about twenty and in college.

"I don't do school," he told her. "I board from March till December and then surf the North Shore all winter."

Blair shoved a potsticker in her mouth and chewed. "How can you snowboard all summer?"

"Chile. Argentina."

"And the North Shore is in Hawaii, right?"

Don't ask how she knew this. It was the kind of thing a girl with brothers just *knows*.

The guy nodded. "You surf?"

Blair shook her head, intrigued by the idea. She envisioned herself in her new pink Eres bikini and a Hawaiian lei made of white orchids and red hibiscus blossoms, balanced on a surfboard and riding out a humungous wave. She'd have an amazing tan and incredible butt muscles—the kind that actually look good in a thong. And after a long day of surfing, Erik would massage her with coconut oil and feed her the fresh fish he'd caught that day. Maybe she didn't really need to go to Yale or any college at all—she could just . . . *surf*.

Nate got up all of a sudden and walked over to her. His emerald green eyes weren't sparkling so much as smoldering. He looked like he had a lot on his mind.

"Hey," he said.

"Hey," she said back. "How come you're not in the hot tub?"

Nate shrugged. "It's too hot?"

Blair jumped up and dumped her paper plate in the trash. She didn't like making small talk with Nate when Erik was outside with Georgie and Serena. It didn't make any sense. "Come on," she said, leading the way outside.

"Catch you later," the stoned guy called after them.

It had snowed for a few hours earlier in the day, and Georgie's backyard sparkled in the moonlight with crisp, fresh, dry snow. No Doubt had morphed into Missy Elliott, and the ski patrol guys were dancing with a group of girls from the local high school on the deck surrounding the hot tub.

Serena had always loved soaking in hot tubs outside at night in the cold, especially when it was snowing lightly and everyone was naked. This time she was particularly grateful to be wedged between her brother and Chuck Bass, while Jan-the-Dutch-dentist gazed at her dreamily from the other side of the tub.

Georgie had eaten too many potstickers or too much something and was doing handstands in the middle of the tub, leaving no part of her naked body up to anyone's imagination.

"Oh," Blair said, anxiously surveying the scene. Okay, so she'd been planning to get naked that night, but not in front of Nate and Georgie and the Sun Valley Ski Patrol and the entire Dutch Olympic snowboarding team. And she certainly wasn't doing any fucking handstands.

"You coming in?" Erik called from inside the tub.

Serena blinked water out of her long, dark lashes. "It's nice."

Blair pulled the sleeves of her borrowed sweater down over her wrists. "Not right now."

Georgie popped up out of the water and wiped her nose.

Her skin was ghostly in the moonlight. "Leave her alone. Maybe she has her period."

Blair blushed angrily.

"Does Nate have his period, too?" Chuck taunted.

Nate pulled a pack of cigarettes out of his shorts pocket, lit one, and then handed the pack to Blair. Then he trudged off into the dark, snowy lawn behind the house, wearing only his sweatshirt, shorts, and tennis shoes.

Blair put a cigarette in her mouth, wishing she didn't feel quite so sorry for Nate. It was weird, this sympathy-for-Nate business. And probably totally undeserved.

"I'm going back inside," she said pointedly.

Serena elbowed Erik in the ribs. "I think that's your cue."

Behind her, Blair heard someone splash out of the tub. "Oh, wow!" she heard Georgie squeal, and knew she was looking at Erik.

Sorry, babe. He's spoken for.

"Wait up, Blair."

Blair stopped in the kitchen and snatched a chocolate macaroon from off the caterer's tray. She took a bite and then turned around to face Erik. He was wearing only a white towel, just like when she'd first seen him at the lodge, the day they'd arrived in Sun Valley and she'd realized that he was the man to deflower her.

Now was as good a time as any.

She grabbed a bottle of chilled Veuve Clicquot champagne from the kitchen counter, tucked it under her arm, and picked up the plate of macaroons. "Let's take these upstairs."

just like santa's reindeer

"I don't wanna go inside," Georgie pouted as the high-school girls and the ski patrol guys followed Conrad, Josef, Gan, and Franz into the house to get something to eat. "I wanna do something *wild*."

Serena's skin tingled. *Me too! Me too!* She was tired of tagging along with Erik and Blair's little lovefest. And she couldn't wait to escape Jan's lovelorn gaze. It was time for an adventure.

"Did you see? Those guys have one of those ski patrol toboggan things on top of their car. I've always wanted to ride in one of those. . . ."

Georgie was out of the tub before Serena even finished her sentence. "Come on!" she cried, stepping into her moon boots, the rest of her just as naked as ever. "Let's check it out!"

Leaving their clothes behind, Chuck and Serena followed Georgie out to the car-filled driveway in front of the house. Quickly and quietly, Chuck and Georgie unhooked the toboggan from on top of the ski patrol guys' Subaru wagon and lowered it onto the snow. Georgie opened the back door of one of the Dutch Olympic snowboarding team's Mercedes SUVs and groped around inside.

"Anyone want one?" she called out.

"Me!" Chuck replied, joining her.

Serena didn't know what Georgie was offering, but she didn't need anything at the moment except a warm coat. "Aren't we going to be cold?" she ventured. The toboggan had a thick wool blanket strapped to it, but unless they all got under it they were going to die of hypothermia.

"Don't you want to be in the papers again?" Chuck wheezed. It sounded like he was snorting something.

Georgie pulled her head out of the SUV and slammed the door. She rubbed her nose, her brown eyes wide. "All we have to do is keep moving." She pointed at Serena. "You get into the sled and Chuckie and I will pull you—like Santa's reindeer!"

Not one to poop on anyone's party and eternally grateful that Jan-the-dentist was too much of a wuss to join them, Serena undid the straps holding the blanket down to the toboggan, wrapped the blanket around herself, and then lay down in the toboggan. Georgie crouched beside her and tucked Serena's arms into the blanket. Then she buckled up the straps, pulling them tight across Serena's body, as if her bones were all broken and needed to be held together. Serena noticed tiny beads of sweat on Georgie's upper lip and forehead, even though it was only twenty-eight degrees and she was naked.

"Ready?" Georgie shouted, her moon boots ankle-deep in snow.

It felt odd and a little scary to be strapped in lying down. Serena couldn't undo the straps even if she wanted to. Underneath the blanket, she pressed her palms against her thighs to steady herself. "Ready."

Georgie and Chuck giggled as they tugged on the toboggan's harness, their naked butt cheeks straining with the effort as they dragged it down the driveway and onto the snowy shoulder of Wood River Drive.

"Wait, where are we going?" Serena called out helplessly. She lifted her head to see, but all she could make out were two naked bodies gleaming in the moonlight as they jogged down the quiet road. Chuck had a tan line left over from Christmas in St. Barts, but Georgie was as pale as a daisy.

Though not nearly as pure.

Serena's neck was aching and she was about to let her head fall back, when Chuck and Georgie's bodies were set aglow by headlights. A car was coming.

"*Help!*" Serena cried, her face aflame at how pathetic she sounded.

Never mind how strange the sight must be.

"*Woo!* Nice ass!" someone shouted out the window as the car screeched past.

The toboggan bumped and slid along as the car's taillights disappeared down the road. "Hey, you guys!" Serena yelled, straining her neck. "Can you stop?"

Her so-called friends didn't even turn around. Perhaps they didn't hear her, or maybe they were just pretending not to hear.

"*Please?*"

But still they didn't stop. The road lit up again as another car approached. This time the car slowed down. Then a siren blared, and red-and-white lights whirled and churned up the night.

"Fuck, it's the police!" Chuck shouted. "Run!"

"No!" Serena shouted back. The toboggan bumped and slid as the police car drew closer.

"Let go! Let go!" Serena heard Georgie scream.

All of a sudden, the toboggan zigzagged haphazardly, before careening into a ditch. It rolled once and fell on its side in a stream of freezing slush. Water seeped through the wool blanket and covered her knees. It was so cold, it felt hot.

"Stop! Stop right there!" the police ordered as they gave chase, the lights on top of their car whirling off into the distance.

Serena shivered in the ditch. The police hadn't seen her.

"Help," she whimpered. "Please, help."

to do it or not to do it

"Now we're dressed exactly alike," Blair said as she stepped out of Georgie's mom's bathroom, wearing only a towel.

Erik put down the ski magazine he'd been reading while he waited for her on the bed. "Cool."

The room had a high, slanted, timber ceiling and gigantic mismatched triangular windows facing Mount Baldy. Headlights on the Snowcats grooming the runs for the following day twinkled in the darkness. Blair wondered fleetingly if Nate was still out there, wandering around in the snow in his sneakers, or if he'd come to his senses and come back inside. Not that she cared. She spun her ruby ring around and around on her finger and shifted her gaze back to the bed. *I'm about to become a woman,* she reminded herself.

Even with cookie crumbs scattered all over his chin and bare chest and his hair damp and matted from soaking in the hot tub, Erik was irresistible. She walked over to the bedside table and took a swig of champagne right from the bottle.

"Okay. I'm ready."

Erik took her hand and pulled her down on top of him. Their lips met in a thrilling mixture of chocolate and champagne. He pressed himself against her hip. He appeared to be ready, too.

She closed her eyes as music filtered up from the party downstairs, some hip-hop song she didn't recognize. The night she'd thought she was going to do it with Nate, she'd burned a mix CD and filled her room with candles. Then nothing had happened. This time she was in a strange house with strange music playing. But maybe it was better this way—the looser the script, the more room for experimentation. Not that she wanted to try anything weird.

Of course not.

"Open your eyes," Erik murmured, nuzzling her neck. "You have beautiful eyes."

Blair opened her eyes and giggled to herself. She was kissing Serena's hot older brother. She closed her eyes again, diving in for another round of mouth-to-mouth. It seemed easier to just do it rather than think about what she was doing or who she was doing it with. Erik pulled back the cinnamon-colored silk duvet and scooted underneath it. Blair shimmied in after him and removed her towel, tossing it onto the floor with more flourish than she'd actually intended.

Ta-da!

"You've done this before, right?" Erik asked as he drummed his capable fingers slowly down her spine.

Blair shivered—partly out of pleasure and partly out of fear—and squeezed her eyes shut. "Oh, sure."

She could feel Erik bulging hugely against her leg. Maybe they wouldn't have to do it all the way, just a little bit. Then she remembered what she and Serena always told the ninth-graders in their peer group. *Don't do it just to do it. Do it with someone you love who cares about how you feel. And don't do it unless you know without question that you're ready.*

That had always been easy for Serena to say. She had lost

her virginity way back in the summer after tenth grade, with Nate, no less. It was the constant, invisible, unspoken *thing* between Blair and her. The albatross in their friendship.

When Blair approached the topic of sex in peer group, she spoke with such authority, she almost believed she'd done it herself sometimes. And sure, she'd come pretty close—with Nate on several occasions while they were together—but not *that* close. She'd always stopped him, just in the nick of time.

Which, considering the fact that she and Erik were both naked and lying *very* close together, was like, *right now*.

"Are you nervous or something?" Erik asked, stroking her hair and looking into her eyes in that pleasant, gorgeous way of his.

"No. Why? Do I seem nervous?" Blair replied a little too hastily.

"It's just the way your knees are kind of pushing me away . . ."

Blair hadn't even realized what she was doing with her knees. Even though she desperately wanted to do it and get it over with, her body clearly had other ideas.

How was she going to lose her virginity when her body wouldn't even cooperate?

her knight in shining armor

Nate was on his way back to Georgie's house, his legs numb with cold and his sneakers soaked through from the snow, ready to give in and jump in the hot tub. He'd thought a good long walk alone would help clear his head, but he had so much to think about—getting into Brown, not making lax captain, Georgie's erratic behavior, the way Blair seemed to look right through him—all he could really think about was how great it would be just to smoke a joint and forget all his troubles.

"Damn," he swore under his breath as he hurried along the shoulder of Wood River Drive.

"Please help?" He heard a tiny, pleading voice whimper from the ditch to his left.

Nate whirled around, his eyes bulging out of his head when he recognized the pale blond hair and the familiar body strapped inside the overturned ski patrol toboggan. If he hadn't been so sober, he would've thought he was having some sort of mental allergic reaction to weed or something.

"Serena?" He knelt down and began unbuckling the straps. "Jesus, what happened?"

As soon as Serena's arms were free she reached up and hugged Nate around the neck, sobbing wordlessly. She wouldn't have minded if it had been Jan who'd rescued her, but Nate was ten thousand times better.

"You're okay. You're okay," Nate murmured, stroking her hair with one hand as he worked the rest of the toboggan straps with the other. When all the straps were undone he pulled back the heavy wool blanket, never imagining what he'd find underneath.

"Whoa." He grabbed her under the arms and helped her to her feet before wrapping the blanket around her once more.

Serena swayed against him, too overcome to be embarrassed or even to explain how she'd wound up naked in a ditch, strapped to a ski patrol toboggan.

Nate bent down and picked her up like an oversized baby. "Let's get you back. All you need is a nice warm bath and some warm clothes and you'll be good as new."

He started down the road toward the house, his arms and legs ablaze with energy from his manly rescue. Serena let her head fall against his shoulder and breathed sweet, warm air into his ear. Maybe it was Nate—her Natie—who she'd been meant to be with all along. Her knight in shining armor. The love of her life.

When they got back to the house, ever-efficient Nate carried Serena upstairs to the guest bathroom and ran her a nice hot bath. While she relaxed in the bubbles, he went down the hall to Georgie's mother's room to look for a warm bathrobe and some cozy cashmere socks. The door was closed, but the cleaning staff had kept it closed ever since he'd arrived at the house, so he thought nothing of opening it without knocking.

Oops.

Nate stood frozen in the doorway, blinking. Blair's clothes were on the floor and her delicate hand with its little ruby ring was curled around the neck of somebody blond. The blond person turned his head, proving not to be a member of the Dutch Olympic snowboarding team—thankfully—but Erik van der Woodsen, Serena's older brother. Which wasn't much better.

"Sorry," Nate muttered. "I just needed some stuff out of the closet."

"Um, can you come back later? We're kind of busy," Erik said, without a hint of embarrassment.

Nate just stood there staring at them with his hands in his pockets. He needed some sort of explanation or acknowledgment from the bottom half of the Erik-Blair nooky sandwich before he could turn his back.

But Blair just lay there with her eyes closed. Erik had almost talked her body into going on the trip she'd wanted to take in the first place, but at the sound of Nate's voice, she canceled the flight. Finally she heard the sound of the door closing and Nate's footsteps hurrying down the hall. Then she rose up on her elbows and inched her body away from Erik's, pulling the sheet up over her chest to cover herself.

"Actually, this was going to be my first time," she admitted, blushing with shame for lying about it when he'd asked. "But I guess I'm not ready." She looked up at Erik, her blue eyes round, hoping with all her heart he wouldn't be too mad.

Erik's adorable lips curled up in a half smile. "Nah. You're ready. I'm just not the right guy, that's all."

And it's no secret who is.

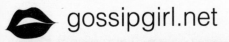

gossipgirl.net

Disclaimer: All the real names of places, people, and events have been altered or abbreviated to protect the innocent. Namely, me.

hey people!

I know, I know, it's seems like forever since we last talked. Spring break is almost over, and by the sound of it, everyone has been pretty busy not thinking about the college acceptance letters that are due in our mailboxes in only two weeks. Yes, we've been busy, busy, *busy*. But before I get down to *who*'s gotten into *what* trouble *where*, let me first clarify a few things in no particular order.

a) The members of the Dutch Olympic snowboarding team are not *all* gay or married or boring. I know this because I hooked up with one of them very briefly when my family was skiing in Banff. His name was Jansen, and he was gorgeous beyond belief.

b) If you are still a virgin when you go off to college, you won't be the only one. I know this . . . well, just because I know.

c) It is not a federal offense to drop mail into a river, unless you work for the postal service.

d) It *is* a federal offense not to answer a girl's e-mail when all she wants is for you to forgive her and kiss and make up. It is also a federal offense to receive a gift and not say thank you. *And* it is very definitely a federal offense to run naked down a public road, especially when the police are chasing you—see news below.

e) Last but not least, as much as I hate to say it, we all feel better about ourselves when we aren't fighting with our parents.

Glad we got that cleared up. Now, the latest news . . .

Infamous Connecticut heiress and Upper East Side boy-about-town arrested for indecent exposure

She shocked us by selling her favorite show pony for drug money, and he shocked us by appearing, all greased up, in a European aftershave commercial. Now they're at it again. **G** and **C** were arrested last night for prancing around on a public road, *in the buff*. It was later discovered that both were under the influence of all manner of substances and that they had also stolen a ski patrol toboggan, which was returned by authorities to ski patrol headquarters. Both parties were released on bail this morning and were flown home to Greenwich and New York, respectively, by private jet. It is rumored that both the Wood River Police Department and the Sun Valley Ski Patrol have already received substantial "anonymous" donation checks to keep quiet about the matter. **G** is already back at Breakaway, where she has earned a lifetime membership. **C** has been grounded, which means he may no longer use his family's suite at the Tribeca Star Hotel or his mother's chauffeur-driven town car. Poor baby. It has also been rumored that a very beautiful model/Upper East Side schoolgirl was involved in the incident, but she managed to avoid the police and escape. Later that evening, a mysterious handsome local boy escorted her back to her hotel. That's our girl!

Sightings

V looking longingly at the film cameras in the window of **49th Street Photo**, like a kid at the window of a pet store. Poor thing can't wait till her parents go home. **B** and **E** and a bunch of **Sun Valley Ski Patrol** guys having a beer at a local bar in **Ketchum, Idaho**, with—believe it or not—no apparent sexual tension. I've heard this can happen to girls once they . . . *you know*. They lose their need to flirt. **J** creeping around the Upper East Side again, hiding behind trees. What's her deal, anyway? **S** and her brother, **E**, tearing up the slopes on their own in **Sun Valley**.

Your e-mail

Dear GG,
I have known a certain boy my whole life and I'm pretty sure I've been in love with him all that time, I just never realized it. He

was with my best friend and now he's with another friend of mine, although I'm pretty sure that's close to being over. I need to find out if he feels the same way about me, but I'm not sure what to do.
—lost

A: Dear lost,
You know what I do when I'm not sure what to do? Grab him. Just kiss him and everything will fall into place from there. If he feels the same way, you'll know. And if he doesn't, you'll know. Good luck, sweetie.
—GG

Q: Dear Gossip Girl,
I love your page. You are a cool girl. I want to find out your name, because I think you may be the same girl I just met skiing. I might never meet you again because I live very far from America, but I will always love you from afar.
—Jan

A: Dear Jan,
I have a feeling we did meet, a long time ago. And even if I'm not the girl you're talking about, you have my permission to love me from afar. But let's keep it that way, okay?
—GG

See you back at school next week. It might actually be kind of nice to sleep in our own beds again.

You know you love me.

gossip girl

it's the thought that counts

When the downstairs buzzer rang, Gabriela and Ruby were making yeast-free, sugar-free, organic whole-grain-and-wild-berry energy bars in the kitchen area of Vanessa and Ruby's small apartment, while Vanessa and Jordy helped Arlo tie the daffodils that he had stolen out of the local park onto the fishing net he'd found and dragged home. Supposedly, the daffodils represented hope, although Vanessa wasn't exactly sure what the fishing net itself was supposed to represent. The net was scratchy and was cutting up her hands, and Jordy was annoying her with the way he was suddenly all interested in her parents and their work. He'd even taken his shoes off when he came inside, just like they did, and he was wearing a beaded peace-sign necklace that he'd probably stolen out of a box of his mom's old things. Needless to say, the sound of the buzzer was a welcome signal to Vanessa to drop what she was doing and *run*.

"I'll get it!" she shouted, stuffing a daffodil into Jordy's helpful hands. She hurried over to the intercom. "Hello?"

"Postal service with a package, ma'am."

Vanessa buzzed the postman in. He reached the top of the stairs and handed over a box. It was addressed to her, and

Dan's name and address were written in the upper left hand corner.

She closed the door and sat down on the floor, tearing open the package with her teeth. Inside, wrapped in newspaper, was a bright pink plastic spaceship with three plastic little girls standing on top of it. The little girls had matching black pigtails and matching green plastic dresses. She turned the toy over and flicked the power switch to on, then set the toy down on the floor. A crazy Japanese dance song began to play as the girls on the spaceship whirled around and around and little plastic lights flashed on and off at their feet. It was tacky and horrible—superfantastically so.

"What on Mother Earth?" Gabriela exclaimed, coming over to look. "Who would send you such a thing?"

That wonderful boy you thought I might marry one day?

"I like it," Vanessa declared. "It's so bad, it's good."

Jordy walked over with a garland of daffodils draped around his neck. He frowned down at the thing like it was supposed to make sense. "What is it?"

"It's just a thing," Vanessa replied, the ideas for her next film already stacking up in her brain. "Hey, could you come down here for a minute?" she asked, thinking of Jordy's nose. He bent down eagerly and she closed one eye, cupping her fingers around the other eye to form a camera-lens view of his astounding nose, the crazy pink spaceship toy whirling and flashing in the background.

Sounds like an Oscar winner already.

"Stay right there." Vanessa sprinted toward her room to retrieve her camera from the closet. If she was fast, her parents wouldn't even notice what she was doing.

"Hold it," she whispered, holding the camera to her eye as she zoomed in on Jordy's nose, making sure to leave the peace-sign necklace and the daffodils out of the frame. "Okay, got it." She turned the camera off and tossed it into her black book bag by the door. From across the living room, her father was watching her curiously, the flashing lights from the toy setting his eyes aglow. She headed back into her room to gather some more supplies. From now on, she'd have to take the spaceship and the camera with her wherever she went, capturing whatever crazy thing she fancied, the spaceship being the only constant, forever in the background.

"Can I stand up now?" Jordy asked when she came back. He was still kneeling awkwardly in front of the spaceship, his eyes woozy from listening to its insane song over and over.

Vanessa grabbed the toy and switched it off, tucking it and her extra batteries and lenses into her bag. "Yeah, you can go," she told him absently.

Meaning she had no use for him anymore.

"Hey, where are *you* going?" Ruby shouted at her from the kitchenette.

Vanessa could already tell from Ruby's tone of voice that her sister knew exactly what she was up to. She laced up her Doc Martens and pulled the black windbreaker she'd bought at the army-navy store on over her head. "Out," she shouted back as she banged through the door, her father's eyes burning curious holes into her back as she went.

the answer may be written
on the bathroom wall

Petite mignonette, sweet coquette
I taste your cookies, your bread
You fill my plate

On his last day at work before school started again, Dan stood in front of the toilet in the *Red Letter* men's room reading and rereading the words he'd written on the scrap of paper that had disappeared from his desk a week ago. He'd found the other poem he'd written using that same last line—*you fill my plate*—and he'd intended to reword the line in this new poem. But it was his fleeting glimpse of Elise holding a baguette that had inspired the poem, and both his interest in her and his interest in finishing the poem had completely diminished.

Did that have anything to do with a certain e-mail he might have received recently?

The redundant line was not the main reason he couldn't stop staring at the words on the bathroom wall. The words he was staring at weren't even his. Whoever had copied his fragment of a poem onto the wall had written underneath it, *Note to self: See above for how* not *to write.*

Okay, so what he'd written was sappy and girly and didn't make much sense. He'd be the first to admit that. But insulting someone's writing so deliberately was just downright . . . mean and immature. It was like talking trash about your mother: Only *you* were allowed to do it.

"Bastards," Dan muttered under his breath as he flushed the toilet. He dug a black Sharpie out of his back pocket and began to scrawl next to his poem.

> *Notes on how not to be an asshole:*
> 1. *Don't steal stuff from people's desks, especially when they don't know you well enough to think it's funny.*
> 2. *Never assume a poem is finished. In fact, never assume anything, because when you ASSuME, you make an* ass *out of* u *and* me.
> 3. *Go fuck yourself, because no one else will.*

He stuffed the pen back into his pocket, washed his hands, and kicked open the door, almost trampling over Siegfried Castle.

"Kid," Mr. Castle addressed him in his awkward German accent. "I am haffing some calls about checks zat never arrived. But you mailed zem yourself last veek. Wusty just called to say Mystewy Cwaze is trapped in Helsinki because Wusty can't wire her traveling money."

Dan walked over to his desk and picked up his black messenger bag. He was tempted to tell Sig Castle that Mystery's check was on its way to Helsinki via the Hudson River, but he didn't want to get fired—he wanted to quit.

Mr. Castle had followed him to his desk and was staring him down with his mean German eyes.

"Why don't you find someone else to be your slave," Dan

hissed. He climbed on top of his chair to read the words written in the red horizontal line that was painted around the room. *Red Letter, Red Letter, Red Letter,* was all it said, over and over. "That's real creative," he added, hopping off the chair. And then he walked out.

Within thirty seconds of his leaving, his cell phone rang obnoxiously in his back pocket. Dan knew without looking at it who was calling.

"Fuck me, kid. NO ONE, I mean NO ONE, quits a job at *Red Letter!*" Rusty Klein shouted at him. "You're supposed to be ABSORBING the aura of literary genius. You're supposed to DO AS YOU'RE TOLD. You're just an APPRENTICE, for chrissakes. You can't QUIT!"

Dan strode up Seventh Avenue South with the phone pressed against his ear, determined not to let Rusty ruin the tingly feeling of triumph coursing through his body. "Sorry, but I don't really get what mailing people's mail or buying caviar or making photocopies has to do with writing good poems."

Rusty was silent—at least for a moment. "Hop in a cab, doll. I'll meet you at the Plaza in ten. I think I know how to handle this."

Dan stood at the head of the stairs down into the subway at Fourteenth Street. He thought about how Rusty had tried to talk him into taking a break from school to write a memoir, which was so totally not what he wanted to do. He wanted to go to college to have new experiences and learn how to write better, and he didn't need an agent to do it. "That's okay, I think I can handle it myself. Actually, I think I can handle *me* myself. At least for a while, anyway."

Rusty didn't answer right away. He could hear the phones ringing and her assistant, Buckley, frantically answering them. Dan waited for her to shout something at him about how he didn't know what was good for him, but instead she just said, "You're sure about this?"

"Yeah," Dan said firmly. "Thanks."

"Well, fuck me. Have a good one, then."

"You too," Dan said earnestly before hanging up. Rusty Klein was crazy and intimidating and kind of a bully, but he would miss her all the same.

He ducked into the donut shop behind him and ordered an extra large black coffee and a jelly donut, dialing Vanessa's number as he waited. His hands shook as he carried the huge, hot cup of coffee outside. He set it on the ground, lit a cigarette, and waited as the phone rang and rang.

"Hey," he said when her machine picked up. "I sent you something. I was wondering if you got it." He took a long drag on his cigarette, trying to think of what else to say. "It's Dan, by the way. Hope you're okay. Um . . . bye," he added, and hung up.

Well, it wasn't exactly "Sorry and let's get back together," but at least it broke the ice.

sometimes the truth bites

Leo was standing in front of the black metal gate, waiting for her. "Hey," Jenny said, her cheeks flushed with the notion that she had invited herself over.

Leo fumbled with the lock on the gate. He nodded at the bike leaning against the metal trash cans in the entryway. "Dad rides that around the park a few times every morning. He's really fit for his age."

Jenny had never even heard Leo mention his father. She'd always imagined him fatherless and lonely in his mother's huge pink-and-white Park Avenue spread, watching TV and brushing that spoiled dog of hers with a gold hairbrush while his mom was out spending the millions she'd received in the divorce settlement on designer dog jackets and dinners with younger men.

"Hey guys, I'm home," Leo called into the apartment as he opened the door. "Here," he told Jenny, taking her black parka and hanging it over his. "Come on."

Jenny followed him down the dark, narrow hallway. The apartment smelled of stale popcorn and Pine-Sol. The white paint on the walls was cracked and peeling, and the plain burgundy rug was worn and linty. It reminded her of her house, only worse.

"Mom, Dad, this is Jennifer, the girl I've been telling you about."

Jenny's jaw almost dropped to her new red suede Steve Madden retro sneakers when she got a glimpse of Mr. and Mrs. Berensen. They were wearing matching gray sweat suits and eating microwave popcorn, their feet propped up on a glass-topped rattan coffee table as they watched TV in their tiny, dark living room. Mrs. Berensen was petite, with short white hair and bright blue eyes surrounded by tiny smile wrinkles. Mr. Berensen was at least eighty, with white hair, long, bony limbs, and a tanned, leathery face. They were both so skinny, they looked like they lived on a diet of only popcorn and water.

"It's really nice . . . to meet you," Jenny faltered. She stepped forward to shake their hands.

"Oh, aren't you a doll," Mrs. Berensen declared.

"We were just watching some old James Bond flick," Mr. Berensen said. "Sit down and watch if you like." He grunted as he shifted over on the burgundy velour couch to make room for them. Jenny didn't know how he could possibly make it around the park on a bike. It looked as if he was going to keel over and die right there.

"That's okay." Leo touched Jenny's elbow. "Come on, I'll show you my room."

Jenny bit her lip as she followed him into the adjoining room. She hated herself for feeling disappointed. Why should she care if Leo wasn't a prince living in an exclusive doorman building on Park Avenue?

Because a guy's gotta have something more than a sweet disposition and a cute chipped tooth!

Leo's room was even more depressing than the rest of the apartment. Just a single bed pushed up against the wall, with some kind of synthetic yellow-and-green-plaid coverlet on it that looked as if it belonged in a motel circa 1979, plain white walls, a linty brown rug, and a scratched wooden desk with a giant Mac on it. The computer was very definitely the newest, most expensive thing the Berensens owned.

Jenny perched on the edge of the bed and sneezed violently. She was having an allergic reaction to this entire situation.

Who wouldn't?

Leo sat down on his stiff wooden desk chair and jiggled the mouse until the computer sprang awake. "This is what I do most of the time I'm not in school or with you."

"Oh?" Jenny wondered if he was about to show her some weird chat room he went to to pretend he was somebody else.

"Come here and I'll show you."

Reluctantly she stood up and went over to look, expecting to have to read through a bunch of annoying e-mails. Instead, it was a painting, an exact replica of Marc Chagall's *Birthday*, with some little flourishes that were all Leo's own.

"You did that?" Jenny asked, when she had found her voice. It *was* very good.

"Yeah, but it's not finished yet. I have to do something about the windowpane. It's a little too bleak." He started opening menus of color palettes and shading techniques. "I could outline it in gold. . . ." He glanced up at Jenny. "What do you think?"

Jenny walked back to the bed again because there was nowhere else to sit. She bounced up and down on it a few times in an effort to clear her head. "I really thought you lived in that fancy apartment on Park. I thought Daphne was your dog." She stopped bouncing, looked down at the rug, and swallowed.

"I guess I sort of wanted you to think that. That's why I took you there."

Jenny looked up. Leo looked a lot less dashing and handsome slumped at his desk chair in his hideous room. "But Elise said she heard you were at that benefit at the Frick. And you have that nice leather jacket." She tucked her hands under her thighs. "I thought that's where you lived," she repeated.

Leo shook his head. "I walk Henry for Madame T after school. She invites me to things like the party at the Frick and gives me memberships to the museums 'cause she knows I like art and her kids are all grown. It's pretty nice of her, actually."

Jenny nodded. Why was it so hard to accept what she already knew? Leo was just a normal boy who walked dogs after school.

And had really old parents and lived in a really dark, depressing apartment. Sure he was into art and so was she, but there had to be more . . . *something*.

Suddenly she scooted off the bed and lunged for the phone. "Let's do something crazy and romantic! We can steal a bottle of wine from your parents and take it to the park and sit out under the stars and get drunk!"

Leo looked dumbstruck. "Maybe *you're* the mysterious one," he remarked with a confused smile. "My parents don't have any wine, and besides, it's a school night. I have to cook dinner and do my homework. You're welcome to stay and eat with us."

Dinner with Leo's emaciated thousand-year-old parents who didn't even drink wine? There was nothing crazy or romantic about *that*!

Jenny didn't know what was wrong with her, but if she didn't bust out of Leo's tiny room very soon, she was going to explode.

"I think I have to go now," she muttered, practically running for the door. Her face was hot, and she couldn't possibly stop to say good-bye to his parents. The front door was only eight feet down the hall. She lunged for her coat, already anticipating the cool air on her cheeks and the soothing bus ride across town.

"Wait!" she heard Leo call after her, but she was already gone.

Elise had told her to figure out if the real Leo was someone she could like. Now she had the answer.

And it wasn't pretty.

b feels the first flush of sisterhood

"It's so wonderful to see you home!" Blair's mother gushed when Blair stepped out of the elevator, wheeling her Louis Vuitton valises. Mookie, Aaron's dog, waggled up to her and rubbed his butt against her knees.

"Fuck off," Blair hissed at him under her breath, even though she was kind of glad to be home. She took off her coat and tossed it onto the antique settee in the corner of the foyer. "Hi, Mom. Where's Kitty Minky?"

Eleanor waddled over and kissed Blair noisily. Then she handed her the phone. "It's your father, dear. We've been having the most wonderful chat."

As far as Blair knew, her parents hadn't spoken to each other—civilly, that is—in over a year. "Dad?" she said, taking the phone.

"Blair Bear," her dad's cheerful, wine-infused voice darted over the airwaves from his château in France. *"Ça va bien?"*

"Sort of," Blair replied.

"Haven't heard from Yale yet?"

"Nope." Blair hadn't given her father any inkling that her chances at Yale—his alma mater—were almost completely destroyed. She wandered down the hallway to her old room and stood in the doorway. "Not yet."

"All right. Well, be nice to your mother. She's absolutely glowing, isn't she?"

"I guess." Blair walked into the room and sat down on the floor. "I miss you, Dad."

"Miss you too, Bear," her father said before clicking off.

"So what do you think?" Her mother walked into the room behind her, breathing heavily. Her stomach seemed to have expanded about twelve inches while Blair was away, but her face was nicely bronzed from the Hawaii trip, and she looked kind of pretty in a dark-green-and-black Diane von Furstenberg maternity dress. Even her black velvet headband didn't seem so bad.

Blair attempted a half-smile from where she sat cross-legged on the floor in the middle of the room. "You look nice."

"No, I mean the room."

Blair shrugged and went back to studying the room. The familiar mother-of-pearl-white walls had been repainted the palest yellow-green, with celery green trim and a stenciled daisy border. Instead of her rose-colored Oriental carpet, a creamy yellow shag rug covered the floor. A bassinet stood in the corner, covered with white lace, and inside it was a folded yellow blanket, stitched intricately with white daisies. Along the far wall stood a changing table and an armoire, both painted pale yellow. To Blair's right was a wooden rocking chair with daisies stenciled on its back. Kitty Minky, her cat, lay curled up on a cushion on the seat of the chair, fast asleep.

Her mother waddled over to the armoire and ran her hand over the drawers. "We wanted to monogram all the furniture, but we haven't decided on a name yet." She smiled brilliantly at Blair. "Your father suggested that you come up with a name. You've always been so creative, darling. I think it's a wonderful idea!"

"Me?" Blair blanched. This baby had nothing to do with her. Why on earth would they want her to name it?

"Don't worry about it being a Jewish name or anything. Cyrus doesn't care. We just need a good name." Her mother smiled encouragingly. "And don't rush into it. Think about it for a while." She walked over to the bassinet, shook out the yellow daisy blanket and refolded it again. "Cyrus and I are going to the 21 Club now for a wine tasting. Let Myrtle know what you want for dinner, and she'll fix you something." She bent down to kiss Blair on top of her head. "Just a good name," she repeated before leaving the room.

Blair stayed where she was, contemplating the color scheme and her new role of Big Sister, Namer of Babies. Her room didn't even smell the same. It smelled new, new and full of promise.

"I've been pushing for Daisy," Aaron said, ambling into the room in a pair of maroon flannel Harvard boxer shorts and nothing else. His baby dreadlocks had grown past his ears again, and his bare chest was tan from his week in Hawaii. He would've looked good if he wasn't so annoying.

"How was Hawaii?" Blair asked, although she really didn't care.

Aaron's dark eyes widened excitedly. "Even better than I thought. I met this girl who's like, even more into being a vegetarian than me. Her parents are Haitian refugees. From Berkeley. She taught me to surf. We had some trippy times."

Blair raised her eyebrows, unimpressed. "But now you're back," she remarked.

He nodded. "So, what do you think of Daisy—for the kid's name?"

She wrinkled her nose. "Duh, Harvard Boy, that's way too obvious." She twirled her ruby ring around and around on her finger. "So what was that Haitian girl's name, anyway?"

Aaron frowned. "Yael. She said a lot of people say it like 'Yai-elle' or something, but she pronounced just like the school: Yale."

"Yale." Blair stopped twirling her ring, the corners of her mouth curving up into a smile. "Yale."

Of course.

s and *n* get it out of their systems

With Blair out of the apartment, there was no reason not to invite Nate over.

"Hey," he said when she greeted him at the door. It felt kind of strange seeing Serena back in her old surroundings. But it was also kind of nice.

"Hey." She kissed his cheek and helped him out of his rain-soaked trench coat, hanging it neatly in the coat closet. His gray Abercrombie T-shirt looked worn and soft, and she couldn't wait to get her hands on it.

"Sorry things got so weird at the party," she said. Thinking about it now, she didn't know why she hadn't kissed Nate back in Sun Valley, after he'd rescued her from the ditch and she was already naked and everything.

Well, she'd just have to get naked again, wouldn't she?

"That's okay." Nate seemed to be waiting for something, like an explanation for why she'd summoned him there.

She took a step toward him, her bare feet cold on the hardwood floor. She was wearing only a thin white cotton undershirt and a denim miniskirt, and she shivered, partly from the chill, but mostly out of nervous anticipation. Nate reached out and rubbed her bare arms.

"Nate?" Serena asked, collapsing into him. She could feel his breath on her face. *Oh, Natie.* "You know how we're always such good buds and we understand each other perfectly and we're always there for each other, even when things get really messed up?"

"Uh-huh," Nate replied hoarsely, still rubbing his hands up and down her arms.

"Well, why can't we just *be together*?"

Nate stopped rubbing. It was impossible even to think of saying no to the most gorgeous girl in his entire universe when she was already one of his best friends and was practically throwing herself at him. Maybe if he just gave her a little kiss and told her gently that it wasn't meant to be . . . He leaned in and kissed her, very tentatively, on the mouth. A nice, sweet, innocent kiss.

But Serena wasn't looking for sweet and innocent, she was looking for true love, and she kissed him back hungrily, like someone who had been waiting for this for a long, long time. She grabbed his hand and pulled him into her bedroom.

"Hey," Nate said, stopping in the doorway. "Is Blair still staying here?"

"Hey," Serena said back, dropping his hand. How could it be true love if Nate was in love with someone else? She sighed and fell back on her bed, smiling sadly up at the ceiling. "Blair moved back home."

"Oh." Nate went over and sat down on the bed next to her. He touched her shoulder. "Are you okay?"

Serena grinned. Even if he wasn't her one true love, Nate was still her sweetie. "Blair and Erik didn't go all the way," she told him, because she knew he'd want to know.

"How do you know that?" Nate asked suspiciously. He hadn't missed the fact that Serena and Blair were fighting.

Serena rolled onto her stomach and buried her face in her arms like a little girl. "I asked him?" Her voice was muffled. "He *is* my brother, you know."

Nate didn't say anything. He was relieved, but he wasn't going to tell her that.

She propped herself up on her elbows. "You know I love you, Natie. But I think we both know who you really wanna be kissing."

Nate nodded and turned his head to look out the rain-spattered window. A big bird was perched on the roof of the Metropolitan Museum of Art. He wondered if it was one of those peregrine falcons that were always flying around Central Park, surprising people by not being pigeons. The falcons were elegant and beautiful, and seeing them every now and again was somehow reassuring.

He lay down next to Serena and wrapped his arms around her in a brotherly embrace. "I love you, too," he whispered in her ear.

Serena smiled and closed her eyes. She could imagine herself and Nate lying like this in her dorm room at college—wherever it was she wound up. They would never be a couple, but every once in a while, they would get together and hug and kiss, just like this. It would always be completely harmless, and Blair would never have to know. And eventually they'd stop doing it, when Serena *finally* found true love.

If that ever happened.

v has more talent than a commune full of hippies

When Vanessa arrived home, Ruby, Gabriela, and Arlo were huddled around the television, eating raw soybeans and drinking warm sake.

"What's going on? I thought you guys were leaving today." Vanessa set down her heavy bag of camera equipment and peeled off her jacket. She'd been caught in a sudden downpour and was soaked through.

"They're leaving *soon*." Ruby clicked off the TV, and the three of them flashed the fakest smiles Vanessa had ever seen. "How was your day, dear?"

Vanessa untied her Doc Martens and kicked them off. From the corner of the living room, Ruby's parakeet, Tofu, squawked inside his cage, as if to warn her, *Something's up! Something's up!*

Gabriela stood up and brushed the wrinkles out of the elaborately printed pink-and-purple Japanese kimono she was wearing. Her gray braids were pinned on top of her head, Heidi style.

"What're you guys still doing here, anyway?" Vanessa asked. "I thought you were going home today."

Her father blew his nose noisily in response. He was

wearing a red wool sweater that had very obviously been made for a woman, because the three-quarter-length sleeves pouffed out at the shoulders.

Vanessa walked toward him, squinting. His face was all splotchy and his eyes were red. "Dad, are you sick?"

Arlo Abrams shook his head and blew his nose once more. Fresh tears spilled down his cheeks.

"Hush, sweetheart," Gabriela whispered, although it wasn't clear to whom.

"It's your films," Ruby finally burst out. She'd never been able to keep quiet about anything. "I showed them your films."

Excuse me?

Vanessa glared at her older sister, too furious to say anything. Then Arlo blew his nose again, his chest heaving with sobs. Vanessa was sort of worried he might be having a heart attack or something.

"Dad?"

"We just had no idea you were so . . . *artistic*," Gabriela faltered. "No idea."

It wasn't exactly a compliment, but Vanessa hadn't exactly been fishing for compliments. Her films were so dark and weird, hardly anyone ever really liked them.

Arlo grabbed the remote and switched the TV on again. They'd been watching the reinterpretation she'd done of a scene from *War and Peace*, starring none other than Dan. The camera followed a scrap of dirty paper being blown by the wind through Madison Square Park at sunset and then settled on Dan, lying collapsed on a park bench. It zoomed in on his face, and Vanessa's heart dropped into her knees.

"Can we turn that off now?" she pleaded. But no one paid any attention.

"It's not just that you can tell a story," Arlo gushed,

entranced. "But the way you do it, like a painter." He turned his teary, bloodshot eyes to Vanessa. "You put us all to shame."

"She got into NYU early, too, cuz she's so freakin' good," Ruby burbled proudly.

Vanessa's face burned. "Shut up."

Gabriela wrapped a tentative, kimonoed arm around her shoulder. "We're so proud of you, Eggplant," she whispered, using the endearing name Vanessa hadn't heard since she was a baby.

Then Arlo came over and hugged the both of them, his face damp with tears. Ruby reached out to rub his back, and soon the four of them were wrapped in a group hug even the hippiest of hippies couldn't top. It was totally un-Vanessa, but it wasn't like anyone was filming it or anything.

"Jordy's going to come stay with us for a while this summer. Is that all right?" Gabriela murmured while they were still hugging.

Ruby snorted. "I don't think she minds what you do with Jordy."

"Oh, I thought you liked him," her mother said.

"I do," Vanessa faltered. And Jordy was nice while he lasted. "I just—"

"She likes that Dan friend of hers from the picture a bit better," Arlo interrupted, as if reading her mind. "He's really got something."

Ruby giggled, and Vanessa kicked her in her leather pants.

Yeah, Dan definitely had something, and she was pretty sure she knew what it was.

Her.

gossipgirl.net

Disclaimer: All the real names of places, people, and events have been altered or abbreviated to protect the innocent. Namely, me.

hey people!

Isn't it great to be back? Isn't it great to be back and *still* not know where we're going to school next year? Isn't it great to be back when it feels like our lives are hanging in the balance and we're all going completely bonkers? Well, here's a little something to look forward to:

Calling all boys

You know you want to meet me, and here's your chance. Tomorrow is our first day back at school, and the weather is supposed to be unseasonably warm and beautiful. As soon as school lets out, you'll find me lying on a red blanket, soaking up the sun on the grass in Sheep Meadow. You are all welcome to join me, and you are also all welcome to bring snacks and beverages. No pretzels or Gatorade, please. Sorry, girls, but this is a boys-only invite. Boys have never been as good at waiting as we are, and you know what they say—the best things come to people who wait.

Your e-mail

Dear GG,
You know that crazy girl **N** met in rehab? Well, I live down the road from her, and we went to Greenwich Saints together until she got kicked out. Anyway, I heard my parents talking about how she was in jail in Sun Valley for indecent exposure, and it's so crazy because her mom was in South America and had no idea she was even there so that kid **C**'s parents had to bail her out, too, even though they didn't even know her.
—Conngurl

A: Dear Conngurl,

That would explain a lot, I guess. And I have to say, **C**'s parents deserve a medal for their generosity. Personally, I think she might have benefited from a few extra nights in the slammer. But what I really want to know is—what did they give her to wear in her jail cell??

—GG

Q: Dear GossipGurl,

ok, so i'm not a stalking pervert, but i did sort of follow this boy i have a total crush on down to s's building and then sat on the met steps in the rain, waiting for him to come out, which he didn't until way after dark and now i have a really bad cold. i feel so stupid.

—atishoo

A: Dear atishoo,

That's a little sad. Although I know which boy you're talking about, and had I spotted him on the street I probably would've done the same thing. What has **S** got that we haven't? Don't answer that—we're jealous enough of her as it is. BTW, I have a cold, too!

—GG

Q: Dear GG,

I heard college acceptance letters are coming late this year because the schools can't decide whether to increase class size or just reject people. They're having a secret forum about it this week.

—ino

A: Dear ino,

I don't talk to people who spread stupid rumors about college acceptance letters. We're all paranoid enough as it is.

—GG

Sightings

B in the **Wicker Garden** buying an adorable yellow cashmere bunny rabbit—probably the first cashmere item ever she didn't a) buy for herself or b) steal. **N** staring up at **B**'s building on Seventy-second

Street like it had all the answers. Don't count on it, sweet pea. **J** and her gangly girlfriend stalking that poor boy from the **Smale School** again. What is it with those two? **D** on the L train to **Williamsburg**. **D** not getting off the L train in Williamsburg. **V** filming new grass growing in **Central Park**—I'm not kidding, she's that serious about her work.

P.S.

I won't totally spoil it for you, but has anyone seen **C** lately? He has a new little friend, and I'm dying to know where it came from. It's so exotic!

See you in the park, boys!!

You know you love me.

gossip girl

why *s* and *b* are still friends

"I made us tea." Serena pointed to the white cups and saucers sitting on her orange plastic lunch tray. She sniffed and wiped her nose on the sleeve of her pale green Calypso blouse. "With honey."

Blair permitted Serena to sit down across from her at the blond wood cafeteria table and accepted the tea. She had a terrible cold. Tea with honey would be just the thing. Besides, she and Serena always sat together at lunchtime, especially when they had peer group, for which they were both leaders.

Plus there was something Blair needed to ask her.

The cafeteria was crowded with girls pouring ketchup over their sweet potato fries and trading gossip about spring break.

"I heard Serena and Nate Archibald got arrested for doing it on a chairlift," Rain Hoffstetter whispered to Laura Salmon.

"I heard she's moving to Amsterdam after graduation. She met this guy from the Dutch Olympic snowboarding team. They're getting married," Kati Farkas told them.

"And Blair's dad is trying to get her into Brown now," Isabel Coates piped up. "Because she and Erik van der Woodsen are totally in love."

"Nothing happened, you know, between Nate and me,"

Serena declared after she'd sat down. She took a sip of her tea. Actually, something *had* happened between them, but that was a long time ago. "I mean, after Georgie's party."

Blair stirred her tea. She and Serena had been ignoring each other ever since the party in Sun Valley, mostly because it was easier and more exciting to let the other girl imagine what had happened than to admit the embarrassing truth.

She pushed her tea aside and rested her elbows on the table, staring at Serena intently. "What was it like?"

Serena put down her tea and blew her nose into a paper napkin. She, too, had a terrible cold. "What?"

"Sex. With Nate."

Serena crumpled up the napkin and stuck it under her tray so they both wouldn't have to look at it. Was this a trick question? Was Blair just waiting for her to say the wrong thing so she could pounce on her with her claws out and rip Serena's head off with her teeth?

"It was really . . ." She paused, waiting for Blair's expression to turn ugly, but Blair just sat there looking genuinely interested. *She really wants to know,* Serena realized.

"It was amazing. We were both kind of scared, but because it was with Nate, it was fun." She smiled, remembering. "And we weren't embarrassed about it afterward."

Blair nodded and looked down at the table. That was all well and good, but what about her? How were she and Nate ever going to do it if they weren't—?

Over Serena's shoulder Blair could see the girls from their ninth-grade peer group heading toward the table. It was time to change the subject. "Never mind," she muttered, grabbing her bag off the floor to get out the materials for peer group.

"Hey, guys, how was your break?" Mary Goldberg, Vicky Reinerson, and Cassie Inwirth asked the two seniors in unison. The three perky freshman girls were all wearing matching black V-neck sweaters. They set their lunch trays on the table and sat down practically on top of one another. "Ours was totally crazy."

"Good," Blair said without much enthusiasm. She gave each of them a handout. "If you could just read this before we get started."

The girls glanced down at the handout and giggled as if to say, *Like we're really going to talk about* that? "So, Serena, did you have to do any modeling over break? I heard you were in a shoot with the Dutch Olympic snowboarding team, like for some lip balm or something?" Mary Goldberg asked.

Serena flashed them a wry smile. The shit people made up about her was so insane, she almost wished it were true. "Yeah, it was awesome!"

The other two members of the group, Jenny Humphrey and Elise Wells, came over carrying their lunches in brown paper bags. Instead of the tired cafeteria salad bar or hot lunch of fish sticks with sweet potato fries, they were eating egg rolls from the Chinese restaurant over on Lex, which they'd had delivered right to the school doors. It was always surprising to discover how crafty the two girls could be when—except for Jenny's gigantic chest—they were the picture of innocence and goodness.

"Jenny is depressed," Elise announced as she sat down. She pulled a piece of shrimp out of her egg roll and popped it into her mouth. "She needs advice. Bad."

Jenny nudged her friend irritably. "I'm fine." She stared at her egg roll, which was soaking, untouched, in a deep bath of sweet-and-sour sauce. After what she'd done to it, it was basically inedible.

"See, Leo turned out to be totally normal instead of a French duke or something," Elise explained, as if they all knew exactly who Leo was, or even cared. "And the only reason he knows stuff about fur and dog boots is because he walks Madame T's dog for her, and we all know she wears a ton of fur."

Blair yawned rudely and dumped a packet of Equal into her tea just for something to do. Hopefully Serena would take care of this one.

Suddenly, Serena grabbed the empty Equal packet out of Blair's hand and wrote something on it. Then she passed it back.

He's still in love with you, Blair read.

The ninth-graders looked back and forth between the two seniors. "What are you guys *doing*?" Mary Goldberg and Vicky Reinerson whined with annoyance at being left out.

Blair folded up the packet of Equal and dropped it into her bag. "So, who here knows how to knit?"

Jenny wasn't sure what the hell was going on. "I do. I learned at arts camp last summer."

Blair blew her nose. "Doesn't everyone learn to knit up at boarding school?" she sniffed in Serena's direction.

Serena shrugged. "I never learned, but all the models are doing it. It's all they do backstage at the shows."

"We've always wanted to learn!" Cassie, Mary, and Vicky piped up.

"Knit?" Elise asked, completely lost.

Blair zipped up her Coach hobo bag and stood up. "Come on," she told them. "We're going out to buy yarn. And after school, we're all knitting booties at my house."

Across the cafeteria, that shaved-headed senior weirdo, Vanessa Abrams, was filming their meeting, a crazy pink plastic spaceship whirling and blinking on the table in the foreground.

Serena stood up and gathered her things. "You mean socks," she countered.

"No. *Booties*," Blair corrected with a smile.

At least it was something they could do with their hands besides smoking. And after school would be a great time to start, especially with the boys otherwise occupied.

The ninth-graders trailed Serena and Blair out the school's great blue doors, thrilled by the idea of being on a field trip led by the two coolest girls in the entire school.

After so many cold months, the warmth of the sun was so intense, it was shocking.

"I'm sorry we were fighting," Serena told Blair as the group of girls walked east toward Third Avenue. "It's not even worth it if we always wind up friends again, anyway."

"That's okay," Blair said, blinking her eyes slowly like a cat in the sun. Maybe it was the weather, but all of a sudden, she felt strangely optimistic. Every day babies were born and given cool names like Yale; boys and girls who were broken up got back together; best friends fought and made up; and people got into college—particularly a college called Yale. "It's such a nice day. I think we'd better go to the park after school instead of to my house."

"I can run home and get a blanket," Serena offered. "We can meet in the meadow."

Uh-oh.

they couldn't stay away

"Fifty bucks says she won't show," Anthony Avuldsen challenged his friends. Nate, Anthony, Charlie, and Jeremy had walked over to Sheep Meadow directly after school let out, just to see if a certain popular online personality was actually going to show her face.

The weather was fine and a bunch of guys were already throwing a Frisbee around. Nate recognized Jason Pressman, a junior from the St. Jude's lax team, and went over to say hello.

"Didja hear about Holmes?" Jason asked. There was a big bag of pot in his lap, and he was busy rolling tight little joints and lining them up inside an old Altoids tin.

"I heard he was missing." Nate licked his lips as he watched Jason sprinkle pot inside a neatly folded rolling paper.

"Busted," Jason said. "Dude got caught in the Miami airport with like, a bale of hash." He sealed the joint and dropped it into the tin. "He's been expelled. Coach says you *gotta* be lax captain now."

Anthony, Charlie, and Jeremy were rolling their own joints just a little ways away. Nate turned around and grinned at them. It was an even better story that he'd given up lax captain only to get it in the end. Besides, he'd earned it.

Jason reached up and slapped Nate's hand, passing him a joint as he did so. "Nice work, man. Congratulations."

"Hey, thanks." Nate held the joint in his fist. "What a day," he observed, throwing his head back to catch the sun.

Good thing there were more guys around than girls, otherwise the grass would've been wet with drool.

The meadow was filling up with private-school boys pretending they just happened to all be in the park at the same time for absolutely no reason. Chuck Bass was sitting cross-legged on a red camping blanket, wearing a black baseball cap with *Sun Valley Ski Patrol* printed on it. Perched on his shoulder was a small white monkey.

Yes, that's right. A live one.

Chuck was an asshole, but he never ceased to entertain. Nate was too intrigued not to check it out. He lit the joint Jason had given him and walked over. "What is that, anyway?" he asked, sucking on the joint.

"A snow monkey. From South America." Chuck scratched the monkey under the chin while the monkey looked up at Nate with trusting golden eyes. "Sweetie, meet Natie. Natie, meet Sweetie."

"Where'd you get her?"

Chuck sneezed and blew his nose into a pink silk handkerchief. "*Him*. Georgie's mom sent him to my parents as a thank-you gift—you know, for getting her out of the whole indecent-exposure fiasco?" He stroked Sweetie's long white tail where it draped over his left shoulder, as though he were wearing an expensive fur stole, only it was still alive. "Actually, they have snow monkeys in the zoo right here in Central Park, but they're really rare as pets. Mom thinks Sweetie smells, but I have my own apartment now over on Sutton Place. So I get to keep him."

Well, isn't he just the luckiest?

"Cool." Nate was pretty much over the monkey now and ready to move on to something else.

"Hey, Nate!" Jeremy shouted at him. "This kid's seeing your old girlfriend. The ninth-grader with the huge boobies!"

Twenty feet away, Jeremy, Charlie, and Anthony were talking to some kid with platinum blond hair whom Nate thought looked familiar, but he wasn't sure. He walked over and shook the kid's hand, holding the joint between his lips as he did so, like Humphrey Bogart or something.

"We're not *seeing* each other," Leo insisted nervously. "We sort of met online and then became friends and then—" He stopped and frowned at Nate. "Hey, I never knew she'd gone out with *you*." He shoved his hands into the pockets of his jeans and kicked at the grass. "Anyway, now we're not even talking."

Just then, Serena van der Woodsen and Blair Waldorf walked into the meadow, trailed by five younger girls, including Jenny Humphrey, the notorious "ninth-grader with the huge boobies." The girls helped Serena spread out a huge red fleece stadium blanket. Then they all sat down cross-legged on top of the blanket in a tight circle. Blair handed each girl a ball of pale yellow yarn and a set of pink metal knitting needles.

"First we have to cast the yarn onto one needle," Jenny instructed. She made a loop of yarn, stuck the tip of her needle through it, and began casting on. The other girls leaned in, watching closely.

Not fifty feet away, Nate continued to puff on his joint. "But you *like* her. I mean, admit it. She's pretty hard not to like."

Leo blushed. "Yeah."

"So what are you doing? Why don't you just walk over there"— Nate pointed to the circle of girls on the red blanket—"and kiss her? That's what I'd do." As soon as he'd said it, he realized that was what he needed to do with Blair—just walk up and kiss her. He'd been horny the whole time he'd been off pot, but when he was stoned he was *romantic*. It was one of the things Blair loved about him.

"I don't know," Leo said quietly. "Maybe some other time."

"Yeah," Nate agreed. Now really wasn't such a good time.

The five boys were still watching the group of knitting girls when Dan walked up, looking ragged and overcaffeinated as usual, a damp Camel dangling from his pale, trembling fingers.

"Hey, did you and my sister break up or something?" he asked Leo.

Leo looked at him helplessly. "I'm not sure."

Dan swiveled his scruffy head around to check out the scene. His classmate and Asshole Extraordinaire, Chuck Bass, was sitting on the ground with a white monkey on his shoulder. Chuck had even brought the monkey to school with him that morning, but the teachers had made him take it home. Then Dan saw something that made him drop his still-burning cigarette in the wet grass.

Vanessa was kneeling on a red blanket ten feet behind Chuck, her face obscured by her camera. In front of her was the pink plastic UFO toy he'd sent her, whirling and blinking crazily on top of a little fold-up stool. Dan could just make out the crazed Japanese pop song emanating from the toy, and it made him want to dance a happy little jig.

Not that he was about to go ahead and actually *dance*.

Nate sucked at the dregs of his joint and nodded at Vanessa. "Think that's her?"

"No way," Dan said. Although he secretly wondered if Vanessa might be the sexy Web mistress they'd all come to see. It would be just like her to do something totally out of character like that and freak everyone out. "Maybe she's not coming."

Nate flicked the dead roach in Chuck's direction. "Not unless she's already here."

The six boys contemplated Chuck for a moment, chuckling to themselves. Despite the fact that this seemed to be a boys-only nonevent, there sure were a lot of girls around. Kati Farkas and Isabel Coates had wandered up to pet Chuck's monkey and spy on Blair and Serena's little knitting group.

"What are they doing?" Kati whined. She scratched Sweetie behind the ears, and the monkey bared his teeth.

"He has sensitive ears!" Chuck warned.

"Maybe they're knitting things to hide drugs in. I've heard smugglers use babies to smuggle drugs into other countries," Isabel suggested, wishing desperately that she could join the circle.

"Don't you love how everyone's looking at us like we're . . . witches or something?" Serena whispered.

The other girls giggled conspiratorially.

Blair wiped her nose and reapplied her lip gloss. She hadn't missed the fact that Nate was among those watching. "They have no idea," she agreed, even though she and the rest of the girls in the group were absolutely eating up the attention.

Her stepbrother, Aaron Rose, came over with his guitar and sat down on the corner of the girls' blanket.

"What should I play?" he asked them.

"*Anything.*" They were all just getting the hang of knit-purl-knit, but the music from Vanessa's crazy pink plastic toy was driving them insane.

"*Stir it up, little darling, stir it up—*" he began, singing his favorite reggae song. Aaron had only turned up to see if Blair was the girl everyone was making such a fuss over. For all he knew, it could have been any one of them.

"You never know," more than one of the boys in the meadow observed.

That's right. You never know.

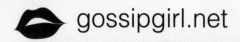

gossipgirl.net

topics ◀ *previous* *next* ▶ *post a question* **reply**

hey people!

About last night

Sorry boys, but you got punk'd! I know it was totally mean of me not to reveal myself, but admit it, you bonded, and wasn't it fun? Just what you needed, right? Best of all, you got to pet that sweet little monkey. And though you hate to admit it, you kind of like that you still don't know who I am, because you *love* imagining what I look like. I'm the girl of your dreams.

What we don't know and are dying to find out

Will **N** and **B** get back together?

Will **S** find someone to love?

Will **V** and **D** forgive each other and live unhappily ever after?

Will we hear more from **G**? Do we want to?

Will **J** and **L** figure it out? Does she want to?

Will **C** come out?

Will I?

You know I can't wait to answer all of the above. But first, I'm building an altar to the Saint of College Admissions. Every day I will buy the saint a new gift, like that pair of beaded slip-ons I've had my eye on in the Barney's shoe department, or that hot pink bag everyone's talking about and no store seems to have. That way, if I don't get in to my number one school I'll have lots of consolation prizes. And if I do get in, I'll have an excuse to congratulate myself with even more gifts. Either way, I won't lose. None of us will!

You know you love me,